Lightning in the Snow

A Collection of Short Stories

VIRGINIA BABCOCK

iUniverse

LIGHTNING IN THE SNOW
A COLLECTION OF SHORT STORIES

iUniverse books may be ordered through booksellers or by contacting:

iUniverse
1663 Liberty Drive
Bloomington, IN 47403
www.iuniverse.com
1-800-Authors (1-800-288-4677)

ISBN: 978-1-4917-9709-9 (sc)
ISBN: 978-1-4917-9710-5 (e)

Library of Congress Control Number: 2016907356

Print information available on the last page.

iUniverse rev. date: 05/23/2016

1

Lightning in the Snow

I should have known when I saw the lightning that this was no ordinary night. Now, the appearance of lightning can be called ordinary. After all, everyone has seen lightning. Thunderstorms are common, even in deserts, but this lightning was different.

The day started out like any other winter day for me. I got up, showered, ran a few errands, and headed to work. I commute an hour each way, so I've learned to enjoy the ride. However, what I like best about my daily commute is that most of it is well, nightly. I work swing shift, so I have the privilege of driving around in the dark after work to get home. Most nights I get to see spectacular moonrises and starlight, and in the summer and fall, any brush fires in the mountains along the route light up my night sky.

I drive along Interstate 15/84 in northern Utah. Utah is mostly desert, but perched smack in the middle of the northern desert lies the Great Salt Lake. It may be salty, but it's still water. And, due to its placement at the lowest elevation in its valley in the Great Basin, it makes finding places to put major highways a bit tricky. Due to this, a large chunk of I-15/84 runs along its eastern border from the northern portion of the Wasatch Mountains. South of Brigham City, the freeway looks west across the lake to the Promontory Mountains, which jut out into the lake. That night, hemmed between these two sets of rocky barriers, I saw the lightning reflected on the vast expanse of water.

Lightning was actually the last thing I expected to see. I'd seen Aurora Borealis in the Utah sky before and often saw shooting stars and plenty of thunderstorms on my nightly journeys. But that night, I saw lighting without a thunderstorm. I saw lightning in a snowstorm.

It was beyond fire and ice. As I traveled north on the sparsely filled freeway, to my left, above the lake, there was a break in the overcast sky. The lights of civilization reflected down on me in purple rays from the underbellies of great, snow-filled clouds. Midway between two giant clouds just beginning to spew swirling flakes, I saw a chasm of black, star-studded sky. As the snow began to fall to the earth in earnest, the great crack widened and ferocious bolts tore though it. The eerie purple-grey light changed into bright white for the second it took for the great bolts to strike the water.

The snow thickened. The purple sky faded into black as my headlights illuminated the frenzied flakes spinning towards me. Familiar landmarks were obliterated. Soon, only the slick silvery surface of the concrete pavement punctuated by the familiar yellow and white lines closest to me remained visible. Sporadically the murk to my left went from gray to silver-white as more bolts connected with earth.

Traffic thinned even more and then disappeared. I felt alone on the freeway, as the lightning continued to burst into my corridor. Suddenly, I was alone. For the last few miles, I hadn't even seen tracks of other cars in front of me. The white stuff was sticking to the cement and asphalt in earnest now. Thankfully, my four-wheel drive truck had new tires; I was able to retain control of my vehicle as I made my way home. As I relaxed into a cautious, snow-driving mode, another lightning bolt struck nearer to me than before. For a moment, the snow ceased. In the split-second of clarity, I saw a silver Chevy truck pulled way off the right side of the road in front of me. I wasn't alone after all.

A strong impression came over me telling me to pull over and try to help. I let my foot off the accelerator to let the truck slow naturally. I knew braking could send me off into a skid. Soon enough I pulled in behind the silver truck. Snow coated it, and I could see the right-rear tire was flat; the rubber tread had separated from the sidewall and the rim sat on the pavement.

The emergency flashers were on, but growing ever more faint. The truck must have been there for a while, snow was two inches thick around it, but I could see bare pavement under it. I was about to pull away and leave, thinking that apparently whoever had been driving had gone for help— when the interior dome light came on.

I normally know better than to stop and help people under my usual circumstances. Freeways are notorious hunting grounds for predators, and I was a lady driving alone, but a warm feeling came over me. I had to stay. Through the rear window the light illuminated what looked like a masculine head and shoulders in the driver's seat. We were still ten miles from Tremonton, the nearest town, and the last car had passed me going the other way twenty minutes before. If this guy was to get any help tonight, I was it. I leaned down to scoop up my cell phone as from its usual charging place on the floor of my truck and tucked it into my parka pocket, thinking I may need it to call for help. As I swung upright and opened my door, the door of the Chevy opened.

Long denim-covered legs slid out terminated by dark work boots that landed in the snowy slush. Matching long arms led a broad-shouldered, lean hipped torso down and away from the truck as the man stood up, shook, and huddled his long coat tighter about him as he hurried his way towards me. I closed my door, rolled down my window, and jacked up the heater as he approached. I'd noted the "BE" on his license plate, and realized he was from my own county, the county we were in.

He stopped at my window saying, "I'm so glad you stopped. Nobody's been past since the tire blew, not even a semi. Can I get a ride into town?" as he looked into my face. The clearest, gray-silver eyes I'd ever seen pinioned me. Snow was sticking in his dark hair making it start to curl at the ends a lot like the warm blood that started curling through my veins. He continued, "My brother is working the night shift at GSTP and I can borrow his truck to come back here, but I need a ride." He rambled on, "The heater blew yesterday, and I haven't had time yet to get it fixed." His last words were lost between his chattering teeth. His leather work-gloves and denim jeans couldn't possibly have kept him warm for long.

I believed him. I knew the Golden Spike Travel Plaza (GSTP) well, knew that it was less than fifteen miles from where we sat, and the vibes told me this guy was legit. "Get in, I'm heading that way. I need to stop at GSTP for gas anyway." I said as I motioned him to get in my truck. GSTP was one of the two main truck stops nestled at the junction between I-84 and I-15 at the northwest edge of Tremonton. I went there often, due to its strategic location at my exit. And coming home at one AM most nights, I had made a regular habit of gassing-up there where I knew the people.

The stranger hustled around the front of my truck and hauled himself up onto my passenger seat. His knees were bunched up nearly touching the dash as he yanked the gloves off his hands and held the numbed digits up to the heater vents. "Thank-goodness." came out of his mouth as he took a deep breath of warm air. I popped the heater button up to the highest notch as I noticed the ring-less left hand nearest to me. After a second, he glanced over to me as I backed the truck up a little and pulled back onto the freeway.

Damn, I knew it. He's checking me out. I thought as I felt his frank appraisal take in my flyaway curls and my own denim-clad right leg. I saw him notice that my seat happened to be pushed back nearly as far as his own for my own long legs. It took a few seconds for his gaze to travel from hip to toe. Thank goodness, he couldn't see my chest or the rest of my body through my coat and arm. I didn't want to be ogled. "What happened to your spare?" I asked as I turned towards him trying to break his staring look.

"Would you believe that my left tire blew last week and that's where my spare is until payday?" he blushed and swallowed hard. "I know, don't say it. My dad's been ragging on me for a month to get new tires, but I wanted to wait for my tax refund." he sighed. "Oh well, lesson learned."

At his abashed tone, I smiled at him. "Don't be so hard on yourself. You'd die if you'd seen the rubber I got taken off this rig just last week. *My* dad about threatened me with my life if I didn't get them changed. I was hoping to wait for spring when they'd be cheaper." The ice broken we turned and met matching, smiling glances. The random thought, *Shit, pinioned again by those incredible gray eyes.* rang in my brain.

Out of the corner of my eye, I saw him continue to look at me. I thought, *Heaven, help me, he's gorgeous.*

His nicely shaped lips opened, "So, what's your name? I'm Jared Comstock. Doesn't your husband hate you driving around at night in this stuff?"

I inclined my head towards him, keeping my eyes firmly on the swirling mess ahead and waved my own naked left hand at him. "It's Gina Anderson, and there's no husband to worry, but my parents care plenty. However, I do this nearly every day. I work nights so I drive along here all the time, rain or shine. Hence the truck for wintry commutes like tonight."

He continued to look at me interestedly, "How far do you have to go, I mean I-84 is freeway, but there's not much traffic north of Brigham. What would *you* do if you had been out there tonight like me?"

I looked at him and smiled and replied, "Well, I'd call the family on my cell phone and sit and wait. However, tonight, I'd have gotten really wet and very cold, as I'd changed my tire. I can't stand running on a spare." I couldn't resist the jibe. To soften the bow, I added, "Besides, I'm a pansy. So when my heater goes out, the truck stays at the dealer to get fixed, and I borrow a rig." I couldn't help but smile at him.

Jared had the humor to place a nearly warmed hand across his heart, "You wound me to the quick." At that, we both laughed.

Luckily, we were near the first Tremonton exit. *Good, only four more miles to go to the second exit and GSTP.* "Are you getting warm yet? I mean you'll take one heck of a chill if you go back out there in this." I asked. I then blurted out, "I mean, I stop at GSTP all the time, and with all those windows, that gas station is never warm enough." That made me think, *Has the blood pumping through my body bypassed my brain? Quit chattering.* I stared directly ahead, glad for the green dash light that hid the flames in my cheeks better than daylight.

Jared seemed to enjoy my discomfiture, because I heard laughter in his voice when he said, "Well honestly, I have on thermals and wool socks, so I'm not too chilled except for my fingers." He smiled and raised an eyebrow and sent me as a flirtatious wink as he said, "Can you warm them up for me?"

Before I could shoot him down by saying no, he grabbed my right hand off its "two o'clock" position on the steering wheel and grasped it between his own cool fingers. What few thoughts occurring in my brain were condensed into, *Good God what's he doing!* and *Nope, there's definitely no blood coming up here into my brain.* My shocked stare met his sparkling eyes under the still-raised brow.

He said, "Yup, as I figured. They're warm and soft. Besides, your truck is an automatic. No sense wasting a hand on the steering wheel when it doesn't have to shift and could be over here with me."

My delighted senses reveled for a moment when, all of a sudden, my beleaguered brain woke up. Regardless of where the blood may be going, *I* was still in charge. I exclaimed, "Are you serious? I don't even know you, and now your holding hands! Besides, I am four-wheeling it on snow-packed roads here." Within a scant twenty-minute period, I was letting this gorgeous hunk of male hold my hand. *Jiminy Christmas!* Echoed in my skull as he leaned even closer and said,

"You haven't pulled it away yet, Gina."

He let go as I belatedly yanked my hand away and pointed to the upcoming exit. I thought, *Thank heavens.* but said, "Here you are." in my best business voice.

"Actually," he started with a tone that sounded suspiciously serious to me, "I was going to ask you if *you* could drive me back to my truck with my brother's spare. I mean he can't very well leave the station unattended, and you're doing fine driving your rig in this muck." He continued speaking and not looking at me as I gently turned into the exit lane keeping my speed down so my traction would stay high. "His truck doesn't have four-wheel drive and it's a pain to get it across town in snow like this let alone trot down the freeway." He went on, "But wait, I don't know how far you have to go. Never mind. I'm sorry. You need to get on your way; your family will be worried."

The warm vibes that had made me stop when I initially saw his truck kicked on again. Deep down, I knew that I couldn't let him go like this. I had to help him, and that meant staying with him. Just then, we arrived at the cattle guard at the freeway exit, decision time—The bright lights of GSTP's parking lot beckoned through the snowy swirls.

Jared must have been considering the situation and somberly too, because his gaze jerked to mine as I made my offer,

"I just live west of town, and my family is probably asleep. They consider no news from me good news, so it won't matter if I'm a bit late. It's no problem, I can take you back to your truck."

"Do you mean it?" he asked hopefully with a big grin that showed two adorable dimples in the stubble covering his cheeks.

I smiled again and the warmth between us was restored. Damning the giddiness swirling inside me that matched the snowflakes, I grabbed his hand and surrendered to the storm. We stopped quickly at GSTP. I pulled up to the pump and Jared said, "Stay in the truck and I'll pump your gas." He was out of the truck before I could stop him.

I opened my door and tried to beat him to the pump so I could swipe my debit card. Somehow he beat me there and blocked me from the card reader. I complained, "I can buy my own gas."

"No dice, sister. I'm buying this tank to pay you back for helping me in advance." he replied.

"But, I need to run premium this tank." I said, worried about him paying so much. My truck had a normal truck-sized tank, but got sixteen miles per gallon (MPG) on the highway, but it was more like thirteen MPG when I used four-wheel-drive.

"I can handle that. So are you going to freeze out here with me?"

I answered, "I can. I'm a bit warm after being behind the heater for more than an hour."

"Okay. After your tank is full, I need to check in with my brother then we can head home to get the spare."

"All right."

Jared lived with his grandfather and brother, only a mile or so from the freeway exit and GSTP. His granddad was away for the week at a cattle auction in Dallas, so at "home" he grabbed the spare tire from his brother's truck. Then he threw the tire in my truck bed and we headed back to his silver Chevy.

I learned that Jared worked graveyard at the steel plant in Brigham City. He'd gone home early that night when they shut down the plant for the storm. But for the snowstorm and that tire, I never would have met him. His shift ended five hours after mine.

I'm sure the lightning I saw in the sky mimicked the lightning that struck our hearts that night, because Jared had also watched the lightning strike in the snow and knew that something special was afoot. He said, "I thought the lightning was a bad omen, because I saw the first bolt and then my tire blew. Of course I had to change my thoughts when you pulled in behind me. I knew watching you drive up, that you were a good driver. But, when I saw you, I knew you were also the girl for me." Jared then lowered his voice a notch and explained, "It was meant to be. Somebody had to help you repent from buying a GMC."

He takes full credit for converting me to "Chevrolet all the way." He jokes about our Chevy lifestyle all the time. My answering giggle always delights him, because he knows the only reason I like going in his Chevy rather than my GMC is the bench.

Those two bucket seats in my truck can't compete with Jared's truck's most comfy bench that allows us to sit side by side with arms and legs touching. What's the point of being struck by lightning, if I can't sit next to the storm cloud that blew into my life as he drives? We spend a lot of time holding hands, but now the fingers are no longer naked.

2

Blessed

$\mathcal{M}$elissa sat on what was supposed to be a comfortable chair outside the Intensive Care Unit (ICU) at Primary Children's Hospital in Salt Lake City. She'd lost track of just how long she'd sat, but glancing at the clock on the wall staring at her, she realized she'd been sitting there for nearly four hours. It was almost six PM, the hospital's dinner hour. Absently, she noticed that the nurses were also changing shift. A platinum blonde nurse named Vickie who happened to look like a six-foot-tall Viking warrior-woman was now replacing the petite Latina pixie Nancy, who'd been so solicitous when they wheeled in her daughter earlier.

The Viking's forceful stride reminded Melissa of Wagner's Valkyries; she seemed to swoop down on the lesser mortals hovering in the hall. Melissa had spent the time waiting to hear more about her daughter's status staring at times across the hall to her daughter Marie's hospital room and at other times at the people around her. To keep occupied, she alternated between imagining impossible identities for the various nurses in the ward and wishing that the horrible throbbing in her left arm would dissipate.

The Valkyrie/Viking nurse was documenting Marie's vital signs. From where she sat, Melissa could just make out the corner of the plastic tent protecting her daughter by looking over the Viking's head. A modified refrain from the song, *Over the River and Through the Woods* flitted through her consciousness, *Over her head and through the door, to Oxygen land we go...* "Great, my baby is lying unconscious across the hall in an oxygen tent, and I'm sitting here singing silly songs to myself."

"And talking to yourself as well." interrupted her friend, Kelly.

Melissa shot up out of her chair. She'd had no idea that she'd spoken aloud or that she'd gained an audience. "Kelly, my heavens, I am so grateful you came!" Kelly Dixon, the neighbor who lived in the other half of Melissa's duplex, embraced her dear friend as tears broke from their eyes. "I had to finish Gerald's cabinets, and then it took two hours to drive down here, but I came as quick as I could. How is she?"

Melissa motioned broadly with her good arm towards the ICU as they entered the alcove next to Marie's room and said, "She's in an oxygen tent. They put a shunt in her right side to stop her lung from collapsing again, her right arm is broken, and she hasn't come out of sedation yet."

Kelly inhaled deeply, "What's the prognosis?"

Melissa turned back from staring at her daughter's tiny body covered by layers of plastic and blankets, "Well, the good news is: it's a clean break—no bones sticking out of her arm. Also, her breathing has improved, and the doctors have sedated her to keep her asleep while they wait for her condition to stabilize."

Kelly seemed to notice Melissa's fragile state and gently maneuvered her back into the waiting room.

Melissa fell back into the stiff chair, remarking, "Thank heaven she wasn't hurt any worse when that semi-truck rammed us. A five-year-old is too little to have to endure an accident like that. I am grateful she survived, but it was awful."

"I agree." said Kelly.

Melissa straightened up and clutched Kelly's fingers to bring her down for a hug. "I am so glad you're here. This is too big to shoulder by myself."

Kelly smiled and hugged her back. "Missy, you know I love you—I had to come and help you. Besides, it's Friday night. We can play down here all weekend! There might even be some hunky doctors around here we can convince to take us dancing in the parking lot." They both smiled at Kelly's familiar joking manner.

"So Hop-along, what's up with that cast on your arm?" Kelly questioned.

"Well, when the semitruck swung over and rammed us into the telephone pole, my left arm got caught between the door and my side. We were stopped at the red light, which was taking forever to change. So, my arm was just resting against the door as we chatted about getting her a car booster seat. That's where Marie and I were going, to get the booster. I just got my taxes done, and my refund is a godsend." Melissa gestured to the thick folder poking out of her purse. "And now I'll finally have enough extra cash to go get a child booster seat for Marie to use until she's big enough to handle an adult seatbelt." At this statement, fat tears started to spill from Melissa's eyes.

Kelly reached over and gently held Melissa's good hand, "Come on, keep going...get it out."

Melissa sniffed loudly, but looked up and continued, "Well, I knew that the rain this morning had made the roads slick, but I had no idea that it was slick enough to cause a semi to lose control. We were just sitting there at the stoplight enjoying the sun peeking through black thunderclouds. Then this speeding semitruck jack-knifed as he came up behind me to turn right. SMACK! It rammed my truck into a telephone pole forty-five feet away across the other lane of traffic and up on the sidewalk." Melissa grimaced at the pain her *smacking* motion had caused in her left fingers.

Kelly deftly interrupted her friend and in a caring voice asked, "Are you sure *smacked* is the best way to describe your day?"

Melissa laughed aloud, "I need your smart-aleck comments today, Kelly. Thank you."

The two friends moved over to the couch where Melissa leaned back to get more comfortable. She said, "Long story short, the trailer crunched my side of the truck, and my arm in the process, as it swung behind us to crumple my truck bed. Then the tractor flew up to the passenger side and slid us across the street and up on the sidewalk where Marie's door gained an eight-inch deep dent *smack* in the center courtesy of Mr. Telephone Pole." Melissa's tone lightened as she finished her statement, but then darkened as she continued, "Too bad Marie's seatbelt never locked." Melissa felt horrified at the seatbelt failure and Kelly looked as horrified. "Kelly, she's too little. She didn't weigh enough to lock the shoulder strap on the front seatbelt. I even saw her little body fly forward. I didn't know why until the cops had cut us out and explained it."

Melissa digressed in her agitated state, "Did you know that they had to use the "jaws of life" on both sides of my truck? Both doors were caved-in and the center console had been pushed up off the floor, so they couldn't pull Marie across to my side to get her out." The tears restarted in earnest. "The only reason Marie wasn't killed by her head *smacking* (Melissa gave the word a nasty tone) the dash when she flew forward, was because my motherly instincts kicked in. I lashed out my right hand and somehow held my baby back against the seat. It's physically impossible that I had enough strength in my arm to do what the seatbelt could not, but somehow it did. Kelly, Heavenly Father must have sent angels down from heaven to hold my little girl in place—she'd have been killed otherwise."

With a sniff and a sigh and four teary eyes between them, Kelly asked, "So, what are the damages?"

"Both trucks are toast. The injuries range from relatively minor, my sprained elbow and swollen fingers and the semitruck driver's whiplash, to my daughter's more serious bump on her head, multiple bruises, collapsed lung, and broken arm. There's also a nasty gouge in my right hand caused by the slipping seatbelt as I held my daughter safely in place. By the way, the cops said my holding Marie back was 'against all the laws of nature'."

Kelly looked over at the angry red welts and cut across the back of Melissa's hand, "Ooh baby. What else did the cops say?"

Melissa shook her head, "The truck driver was in a hurry, of course, and had overestimated just how far he could, as he put it, 'ride the ridges'. So, when his rear tires hit the water pooling in the ruts on the road, he just lost control. It's clearly his fault. He was ticketed, and could lose his license, but I can't worry about him, my baby is my number one priority."

Kelly looked at Melissa, and asked curiously, "You seem nonplussed about the other driver. Man, aren't you ticked at him? I mean his recklessness caused the accident!"

Melissa replied, "Kelly, I agree. I was angry, but I couldn't stay mad. How can I, a speed-demon, possibly condemn someone else for something I do myself? It's not as if *I've* never sped in order to get somewhere on time."

This turn of the conversation sent the mood in the little waiting room in a somber, downward spiral. Kelly looked like she was considering what Melissa said, then said, "I guess you're right, Missy."

Melissa closed her eyes and added, "Besides, how can I waste energy on anger, when my little one is in such danger?"

"So what are your plans for tonight? Can I get you a pizza? Is the hospital going to get you a room?"

Melissa answered, "Yeah, they actually got me a room in the parent's center downstairs, and they offered to bring in a roll-away bed if you want to stay with me tonight. I was waiting for you to come and, yes, for you to get a pizza, but I really need your company."

Kelly cast a concerned glance across the way, "Will she be okay?"

"The doctors said that Marie should wake up just fine, and then they will check her condition to be sure. They were cautious, but when I asked about her head injury, etc., they assured me that she doesn't have a concussion. Dr. Monson actually said, 'She was just cold-cocked. We gave her a light sedative to help her stabilize.'"

Melissa felt a spark of hope as she turned back to Kelly, "In fact, the day nurse Nancy said that they'll start watching for Marie to wake up on her own around seven o'clock. That's why I had you hurry down here. I need to be here when she wakes up and I'd hoped you be here with me. She'll be glad to see her Aunt Kelly—especially when you trot out to Pizza Hut for our dinner after."

The two friends embraced again. They had just settled down when "Vickie the Viking" rushed into the room, gesturing excitedly. "Ms. Walker, come quick. She's awake and crying for you! That little girl is blessed. Her breathing, heartbeat, and vital signs have improved. Dr. Monson says she'll be just fine. Hurry in there, they're waiting for you."

3

Chuck

*C*huck began by writing me love letters. I enjoyed the extra attention he gave me. After work, I would tell my mom and dad that I was just too tired to hang out with the family and go up to my room to read them. I stopped going out with my friends as much. I spent more and more time pouring over Chuck's devoted lines.

I was pretty sure my mom would find out about us eventually. She's always gone through my room snooping. I pretended that the "Chuck" in my journal was actually my childhood buddy, Charlie. As if! My mom knew about my big break-up with Charlie during the sophomore "Freak-out it's Summer" party the last week of school, but I let her think that we made up on the Fourth of July.

Actually, I went to the park with Chuck that night. When I came home after with my first hickey, Mom asked if it was Charlie. I hinted that it was. She seemed to be almost okay with that. Charlie's mom and my mom work together at the grocery store, and they're friendly. She lectured me about condoms, and took me to the doctor for birth control. She was guessing that I needed it. I didn't confirm or deny it. At that time all that Chuck and I usually did was neck a little.

I really enjoyed reading Chuck's love letters. There's something about his devotion in them that worked for me. He swears that he will love only me. The letters made me feel warm all over. But, because Mom is such a prude, I only put some of my tamer thoughts down in my diary. There's no sense in letting her get too worked up.

That's not why I held him back from "doing it", though. He had to get rid of that witch he'd married before I was going to let him try anything. I swear she got pregnant purposely just to make him marry her. But, that's not the only reason that Mom putting me on birth control stirred me up. Chuck had gone a little too far the night he gave me the hickey. We'd been sitting behind the big crowds watching the fireworks. I'd let Chuck kiss me for the first time a few days before, and I liked it and wanted to try it again. His mouth was a lot hotter than Charlie's, and I got caught up in the comparison that night. Now, I'm only putting this down here, because there's no way I can write this down in my diary or talk to anyone else about it. I mean all my old friends hate me, because I've been dating more than them. Besides, they've never had a guy even pet with them, so they'd have no idea what "doing it" is like and they think I do.

Before I knew it, Chuck's hands were under my shirt. I hadn't realized he'd undone my bra either. By the time I came to my senses enough to realize that he'd unzipped my jeans, his thing was pushing against my stomach. I freaked out. I mean I'd never even really seen any guy naked, not even my dad. I somehow pushed him off me. Luckily, the fireworks had already started. So, by the time I got through crying and drove home; it was like I had stayed to the whole show. I had no idea that I had my first hickey until my mom hustled me past Dad and into the kitchen for some "girl-talk" before bed.

I let Mom think that I'd made up with Charlie, because she liked to come see me at work on her lunch break some days. I thought that talking to me about Charlie would distract her from noticing how Chuck would stare at me at work.

She liked to gush about how her and Joan—that's Charlie's mom—have been planning for us to get married, and they were looking forward to sharing grand babies down the road, etc. Plus, I knew that if Chuck got wind of their plans, he'd be jealous, and I'd get some payback.

That Chuck though, he knew he'd messed up on July Fourth. I was pissed. He made up for it big time. I got flowers at work five nights in a row, and to prove his love, he kicked that bitch out. She had got ticked at him for some reason, and he told her to go straight to hell. He even drove me past his apartment, as she was moving out to prove she was leaving.

Once she was gone, while we had more freedom, I had to give up my diary. I'd been trying to find a way to stop making up crap for it. That week I watched Mom real close, and finally, I "caught" her reading my diary. I played it perfectly. My tender heart was shattered. She ate it up. She even admitted it wasn't the first time. I was glad that I was saved from having to make up more mush. I had the real thing.

Chuck and I started going to his place after work nearly every day. I was working every weekday plus some weekends while school was out. First he took me to his house using the excuse that he needed my help to plan the work schedule. Things progressed and we began "doing the deed" whenever we could.

Then in mid-August, I had the next day off to go school shopping. My dad was picking me up after work, and then he'd drive us into the city. Chuck had been getting tenser and tenser the closer it got to school starting. That day I planned to knock off work early so we could spend all day at Chuck's—it was kinda my way of helping him get over his worries about my school. I planned to make it back to work just before Dad got there so I could pretend I'd got off at my usual time. It would be tricky to time it right, but I was determined.

I figured Chuck was worried about school hampering our activities. It was hard to find time to get together unless we hooked up after my work. He knew Dad refused to let me work during school; I could only work during the summer. I also knew the end of our easy time together was coming, and I guess, I wanted to really celebrate.

By that week of the summer, I'd paid my dad back for my car, and gotten a new curfew, but I still had to be home by midnight on the weekends. *I* knew it would work out, but Chuck began to snap at me now and again. I didn't know it at the time, but looking back now I can see his worrying about how we'd function during school caused his temper fits. He always made up for picking on me after, but the incidents were starting to worry me.

I'd started using my birth control pills faithfully after I'd had a small scare. (No, I'm not a mom.) Not that I told Chuck, it was my responsibility to take the pill—he made that clear. So that celebration day, I was on a real high. Not only was my latest pregnancy test negative, Chuck was able to get the whole day off. He planned to make it up by working a double shift later. I barely made it through my shortened shift. I was so excited. As soon as I could, I booked it over to Chuck's.

Unfortunately, my dad had decided to take our shopping day off too and planned that he, Mom, and I would head into the city early and have dinner as well as go shopping. He was going to make a mini-vacation out of it. He and Mom decided to surprise me with this, so Mom packed an overnight bag for us, while Dad got the car ready. Then, they headed to work to get me.

If I had left five minutes earlier, they would have missed me and things would have been okay. Mom told me later that they had a backup plan; if we missed each other we'd have just gone later as originally planned. But, instead, things went all wrong. I had just turned onto Main Street as they pulled into my work's parking lot. I didn't see them. But, they saw me head north instead of south where home was, and decided to follow me. I was far enough ahead of them that they saw which neighborhood I went to, but not which apartment or house.

Now, my friend Angie lived on the same block as Chuck, so when Mom and Dad didn't spot my car right off, they went to Angie's, thinking that's where I was headed. Angie knew about Chuck being my boss and boyfriend. She also knew that we'd have "work meetings" at his house. She ratted me out and told them where he lived.

Dad and Mom pulled up to Chuck's complex. Dad was getting out of the car when Mom grabbed his arm and pointed to the third floor window where Chuck had forgot to close the curtains. Dad and Mom watched Chuck take my shirt off. Of course I wasn't wearing a bra. That did it.

There was a reason I never let Dad know about any of my boyfriends. It was the same reason Mom wouldn't let him see my other hickeys. Dad's temper would have exploded, and I'd have been sent to Catholic school or worse. Dad's little sister had gotten pregnant at sixteen and went from deadbeat guy to wife-beater to a very evil man. My cousin Lacey had been so badly beaten as a toddler, that her face was misshaped. Evil kids used to call her hunchback after Disney's character. So Dad was a little touchy about the idea that his only daughter might one day have sex.

When Dad saw us in the window, he exploded out of the car, and was upstairs in three seconds. Angie, of course, gave him the apartment number, and at a very delicate juncture, Chuck was lifted off me, thrown across the room, and then cold-cocked by my angry father. My dad threw a blanket at me and gave me ten seconds to get dressed. Mom followed in his wake and helped me up off the bed. I was scared, then terrified, as Dad called the police. Statutory rape. No question; no consent possible.

My father taught me a valuable lesson that night. He could be more ruthless to his own kid than to strangers. He told the officers what had happened, happily accepting possible assault and breaking and entering charges. I figured that Chuck would be arrested and that was it. I was worried about him, but it's not like he raped me. I was also very aware that I was now grounded for life.

Stiffly, Dad walked Mom and I to the car. The officer had wanted him for questioning, and Dad volunteered to go to the station after he took us home. I figured we'd go home, I'd clean up, and then Mom would lecture me until Dad got home. I knew my car would be surrendered as well as my TV and computer, but I was too old to spank.

Dad, however, is a smart guy. We pulled into the driveway sure enough, but only Mom was allowed out of the car. My father told me to stay put as he got out to say a few things to Mom. She looked at me with tears in her eyes as he talked, and then went inside. Dad got back in the car, and then *we* went to the police station.

He made them do a rape kit on me. The doctor picked up his disapproving attitude. I would have thought a lady-doctor would have been more sympathetic. I was mortified. I tried to explain that I loved Chuck, but the doctor told me that it didn't matter; I was underage. She tried to soften it, but she finally made me understand what "jailbait" really meant.

I felt like I had hit rock bottom when reality finally intruded on my shame.

At the station Dad had calmed down somewhat. He'd been fined and assigned a possible court date, so he could go. He chose instead to wait for me downstairs by the booking desk. While he was there, he'd overheard an interesting conversation. Dad called Mom to have her call Angie to learn more about Chuck and me. Turns out, Angie didn't think Chuck and me were going to last, because she knew better. Angie's oldest sister Veronica just happened to be best friends with Chuck's wife. They were separated, but had never stopped seeing each other. Angie knew that Chuck's wife had been staying with him off and on, and was in fact pregnant, again. While Mom was sharing this information with Dad, Chuck was on the phone to his wife.

It took my father relating the phone call where he overheard Chuck begging the little Mrs. to come to his rescue, then giving me proof by taking me downstairs to see Chuck's wife post his bail, to make me feel sucker-punched. I wanted to die, or at least to pass out. Worse, I hadn't taken my pill that morning. Chuck use a condom? *Please*. I had two weeks before a preg. test would work. I was sick.

I survived against my own wishes. I wasn't pregnant, though I now have herpes. Angie came over to see me, and we got to talking. Seems she'd had similar fun that summer, only her guy had broke up with her when he asked for space, then went back to Montana. It was good to commiserate with her. I learned she was a true friend after all.

I got to finish high school with the nuns of St. Catherine's. It wasn't that bad really. I kinda miss Charlie though. He'd get me out of P.E. to help on the student council back at our old school. Plus he was my pal. But, no dice. Dad chose St. Catherine's 'cause it was for girls only.

★★★

Well, I've finally turned eighteen and graduated. I'm looking forward to college. That's part of why I wrote this. I wanted to take stock of my life before it changes again.

After I was able to leave the house unsupervised, I got a job at a vet's office. Dogs and cats seemed to be safe territory. Happily, through work I got my scholarship. One day I hope to be a veterinarian myself.

I've seen Chuck off and on since that summer. He's now divorced and working at a gas station after getting fired for being drunk at work after the time he served in jail for my statutory rape. He drove drunk too, and a recent Driving Under the Influence (DUI) conviction broke his probation.

I spend my time after school now a little differently than I did that summer. Besides working at the vet and keeping myself out of trouble, I get to baby-sit my cousins for free. Dad's little sister not being married hasn't stopped her from having kids with all these guys. My dad decided that babysitting her brood would be the best way to encourage *me* to not be a mom just yet. The pictures of genital warts and aborted fetuses on the fridge also help to keep me celibate.

My life would have been a lot different if I'd have stuck to pal-ing around with Charlie rather than playing with a real dog. But, if I had, I don't think I ever would have grown up. After all, I could put Charlie down in my sleep back then. Too bad that I had to learn the hard way about the differences between nice guys and assholes.

However, that awful summer brought our family closer together. I didn't learn how to speak to my dad as an adult until he nearly got me arrested and charged as one. Of course, Charlie has grown up too and lately I've noticed he's taller and started to wear hair on his chin. I've also heard he's noticed how much more mature I am. Don't worry, I won't jump his bones, but maybe it's time I tried dating a nice guy for once. Maybe now that he's older, Charlie's kisses will be hotter.

4

Mona's Daughter

Mona Eckerson sat in her husband of thirty years's BMW while he lay in the hospital across the parking lot from her. *He's on the eighth floor, the terminal cases floor,* the tiny voice in her head reminded her. She'd first been acquainted with that particular floor of LDS Hospital when her sister lay dying of cancer. She could still picture her sister clicking and re-clicking the button on her morphine dispenser on a bad day near the end. Only on the eighth floor were patients allowed the maximum doses of morphine or other painkillers. There, the best nurses watched over the worst patients—the patients who would probably not leave the hospital alive.

She chided herself. She had agonized over Mick's disappearance in the jungles of Viet Nam, and he'd survived. He can survive this. She'd done the right thing. *At least I pray I was right.*

★★★

Lily Eckerson, a twenty-seven-year-old grad student at Boise State, sat at the nicked kitchen table that served as a workbench in the free-standing cinderblock garage behind her rented house. She'd known when she saw the garage that *this* was the house that would be her home for the two years it would take to get her Ph. D. Her woodwork needed an open place, isolated from her bookwork. She'd put off her woodworking while she finished her Masters, and by so doing, learned the hard way that her woodworking, or her creation (as she termed it), was the only way she could survive so much "bookwork."

Now it was time for her summer off time. Normally in June, she always took three weeks off and headed back to the Puget Sound of Washington State. In the sailing vessel she had crafted herself, she would head west, toward home, and glide among the waves. There, she could remember the waves of her past that ran along her grandfather's fishing boat.

Before she left Washington each trip, her brother Tao would chastise her for coming so close to Mother in Seattle and never staying longer than overnight. Lily secretly considered it her right. After all, she had not chosen to be a hated half-creature. Her mother had chosen it for her and caused Lily more pain than she could easily forgive. Lily also knew that by existing, she had destroyed both her and her mother's way of life. The specter of this unhealed rift made it hard for her to visit long. Her mother had doomed her to an existence an ocean away from her home because of blood.

As a four-year-old child, Lily had learned the awful truth. *She* was the reason the villagers would not visit her family. Because her mother had lain with one of the hated American soldiers and got with child, she had been ostracized, along with the child borne of that passion. When the Viet Cong attempted to punish them for this betrayal, Lily's mother fled with her daughter back to her home village near the sea.

Her grandparents welcomed their cherished daughter home, and claimed her child as family—becoming objects of hatred too. Lily, adored by her grandparents, had grown up unaware of this hatred at first. From earliest times, she had been allowed to help her grandfather fish in the wide, blue Pacific near their home. These made up her fondest memories—underscored by her mother's distant attitude.

Her mother Jin had been popular in Saigon. She made good money singing and dancing in the clubs, and by lying with the soldiers, until one of them got her pregnant. Lily's mother felt no shame about her past—the money she'd earned kept her family from starvation.

From the loving, sheltered environment of her early childhood, Lily was plucked up and shipped to the USA. Her mother found a rich Vietnamese man who was fleeing the Viet Cong. He had been hiding in the village, and when he heard of Lily's parentage, used his charm to seduce her mother. Once Lily's mother was firmly again with child, he whisked them away to America, using an old picture of the U.S. Marine and Lily's parentage to help gain them entrance.

He abandoned them in San Diego. Lily was five years old, her brother six weeks old, and Jin twenty-two when they left California for Seattle. That's where Lily finished growing up.

Ironically, she learned of her grandparents' fate from her birth father. About two years after Lily's family had immigrated to the US, her father Lt. Michael (Mick) Eckerson tracked Jin to the village. There he learned her grandparents died in a cyclone during the winter after Jin and her little family left. Apparently, her grandparents had been fishing together, when storm-swollen waves capsized the boat and ran it aground. The villagers were wary of Mick, and only told him of Jin's and his daughter's fate to make him leave.

Six months later, Mick tracked Jin to Seattle. A brief affair had caused a real mess for him, but rather than pretend it never happened, he'd said, "I can't let the war go until I have made amends to Jin and my unknown daughter."

In the drab living room of their latest apartment, Mick met his eight-year-old daughter on a bright Sunday morning. Through a long conversation, Lily was made to understand that this huge blonde stranger was supposed to be her father. When Jin collapsed in his arms crying at the news of her parents' death, Lily's mind could not accept that this monster who had ruined their lives could be holding her mother. She ran at him, pounding, screaming for him to release her mother. When he ignored her, she ran out the door and stayed away until it was dark.

From that time on Lily saw Mick every few months. He and Jin became good friends, though when Lily scrutinized their relationship for any romantic undercurrents, they were absent.

Mick helped Jin get a job as a secretary at Boeing. He also connected Jin with his friend James who had been in Viet Nam with him and had learned Vietnamese. James helped Jin polish her English. Meanwhile, Mick started a college fund for Lily and tried to be her friend regardless of her icy attitude.

When James and Jin fell in love, Mick was the best man at their wedding. That's when Lily met his American wife Mona, and his REAL family. Not that they knew who she was. *Dad let them think they were there only to wish Jim well.*

Lily could admit today, that part of her attitude against her father may have come from her fourteen-year-old viewpoint. At the wedding, she had been devastated and struck with jealousy to see Mick coddle his wife and joke with his teenage sons. It took her a long time to accept James as her father, as she simultaneously tried to accept that her real father had plenty of family without her.

Now in the Boise sunshine, the first smile lit her face as Lily's thoughts continued. James was the only American she knew who *really* understood what Lily's heritage meant. He took special pains to alleviate her fears and show her the worth he saw in her. His unconditional love eventually melted her heart so much that when Angela was born on Lily's sixteenth birthday, she didn't hate her baby sister.

James was the one who taught Lily to work with wood as his grandfather had taught him. Remembering his help, Lily could almost feel bad about her recent unwillingness to stay with her family because of her mother. Through it all,

Lily understood in some part of her that Jin loved her, but the old distance and resentment from the village kept them apart.

Nope, no trip to Washington this summer. She thought. Lily wasn't sure whether she should feel relieved or guilty, but the phone call two months ago changed her life once again. Regardless of how she felt about her father, without helping him now she may never get the chance to make things right with him. Her mother would just have to wait.

A honking horn released Lily from her reverie. Here was the taxi. Reaching down she scooped up her suitcase and her courage, and headed down the driveway.

The flight to Salt Lake was uneventful, even considering the smallish planes that flew between Salt Lake City and Boise. When she exited the gate and made it to the baggage claim, Lily spotted Mona and Steve Hamilton, her father's lawyer, the one who handled her trust fund.

Lily recognized Mona partially by her designer boots and pageboy haircut. Mona had always taken exceptional care of her body, and it showed in her athlete-thin physique. Mona's appearance looked great, but for the first time, Lily saw cracks in Mona's famous composure. Worry lines stamped Mona's perfect countenance, the deepest running between her brows.

Surprising Lily, Mona raced up to her and grabbed her in a firm hug. "I am so glad you made it safe, Lily!"

Lily watched as Mona spotted her oldest son Jason watching them and half-smiled, "Lily, I know this is a bad time, but I must confess that my sons, your half-brothers, do not know your connection to our family." Mona added, "I was upset about you at the beginning, but I've realized that you are the daughter I always wished for but never had. I need you to know that *no matter what*, you are important to Mick and me, and you will always be a member of my family regardless."

Mona turned to her eldest son and with a deep breath and sigh introduced them, "Jason, this is your sister, Lily Eckerson. She is the surprise I told you about. Not only is she more than capable of helping you write your dissertation, she has the matching bone marrow your father needs."

Ignoring the shocked stares around her, Lily wasn't surprised that Mona took charge of the group and headed them out of the airport. She thought, *I bet she decided that it would be better to put out any fires now, before we left the airport. She's probably right. The drive across Salt Lake will give everyone time to adjust to my existence.* Lily followed at the front of the group as Mona steered them out to the parking lot.

In the car, Mona gave an all-encompassing litany: "Jason, before you ask, her birthday is July 23, 1974, exactly six months after your own. She is a Doctoral student at Boise State, and I am glad to have her here, although I could wish it was under different circumstances. Steve, don't say it. I know the boy is shocked. Lily, I meant it. I don't think of you as a blood donor. From the minute Steve confirmed your existence you became my daughter. Finally, Jason, she is Vietnamese. Your father loves me. And, the rest is none of your business."

★★★

From her perch in the BMW, Mona thought about when she picked Lily up at the SLC airport just three days ago. Her sons had almost adapted. She'd had years; they had days to accept their father's infidelity. Besides, although Mick had confessed the affair years ago, Lily had been a complete surprise.

Mona thought, *Has it only been a few weeks ago since I shocked Hamilton so badly by waving Lily's birth certificate in his face?* She had been and was still determined to save her husband from the leukemia he was suffering as a late-occurring side effect from his contact with Agent Orange. Even now, her cheeks flared red at the thought, that she, Mona Eckerson, the picture of wifely obedience, in a fit of mad desperation, had rifled her husband's desk as he lay suffering in a hospital. She'd found not only Lily's birth certificate but the trust documents as well. Relief had swamped her. *All this time, I'd thought Mick had spent his money on gambling or worse.*

Mona gathered herself one more time. *The boys will just have to learn to accept Lily.* Steel formed her shoulders as she thrust out of the BMW and headed into the hospital. "Lily has six weeks of recovery after this, and damn me if I'll let her stay in a hotel." The muttering ended as Mona maneuvered her six-foot one-inch frame down the corridors.

They'd finished the last-minute transfusions last night. Twenty-four hours ago, the doctors transplanted Lily's marrow into Mick. Mona came around the corner and spotted Lily and Jason sitting side-by-side staring into space. *I hadn't noticed, but they have the same ears, Mick's ears.* Her other sons, Matt and Jerry, sat hunched-over side by side across the hallway. None of them had slept last night as they waited for the prognosis. Just beyond her new daughter's shiny black hair, Mona saw the plastic tent encasing her husband. Clutching Lily's fingers and grabbing Jason's arm, Mona and her children entered the ICU area.

Time slowed, hearts pounded, Lily began to sway prompting Mona to grab her waist as the doctor turned towards them. Dr. Hansen looked them over. He noted the black circles under five sets of eyes and their held breath. "Good News!" A broad smile burst across his face as his two thumbs lifted and pointed upwards. "He's gonna be all right!"

5

The Ugly Choices

Geneva shrugged the sweater off her bare shoulders and stretched. Her female parts were stretched and warm from the afternoon's activities. Anthony was so bad for her, but she couldn't seem to help herself—it was great sex. He was the only man who had ever touched her heart. That choice he'd made in a wife was just too bad for him, really.

He'd taken a long lunch today from his job as a foreman at the commercial construction company run by his father-in-law. They'd met at the posh restaurant across from the hotel the company was renovating. Supposedly he was having lunch with a client. Only Geneva knew better. She'd purposely worn this slinky dress with the black silk sweater hiding its allure. Anthony, or Tony, as everyone knew him except his banks and the company's payroll staff, had barely raised his eyes from staring at her legs to ogle her cleavage. Geneva was well aware of her assets. Just because he'd married the mousiest girl she'd ever seen didn't mean that Tony wasn't into long legs and lush curves. Geneva's black hair and green eyes set off by dark gypsy lashes completed the picture.

Just this afternoon they'd laid in the bed together after soaking up the watery sunshine from the hotel windows.

Geneva lay on her stomach with her head sideways resting on her arms. Tony stretched across her back playing with her long hair. Thinking she was asleep he'd muttered out loud, "I wish Rosemarie had kept her hair long, but it was never like this."

It was getting to be too much for Geneva. She'd fallen in love with Tony at sixteen—long before he'd even noticed her in that way. He was the same age and they'd gone to school together ever since their mamas had enrolled them in the same pre-school at age three. Geneva knew how cliché her story was, but she couldn't help it. Tony was still growing into his gawky frame and broad shoulders when her boobs had sprouted and her long legs turned shapely. He'd considered her just a friend and a study partner. He asked other girls to the dances, but took her to the football games and to study groups. Geneva could still remember that day late in senior year when Tony had found her to sign her yearbook and stared at her legs for the first time. It was like he'd never seen a pair of legs before. Granted, she was wearing a black mini-skirt with black silk pantyhose that she normally didn't wear to school. She'd had a college scholarship interview later in the day and wouldn't have time to change. She'd been sitting on the carpeted floor below her locker with a girlfriend when Tony had come over. Of course sitting down like that hiked the mini to the upper mid-thigh zone, and Tony was clearly shocked and interested.

She'd known that that day he'd finally realized that Geneva Scott, the girl who'd got him through Calculus, was a *girl*. Of course, that day it was also too late. He was off to school in the next county. She was hoping to get into the best university in the state—four hours away from their little town. "Hey, let's keep in touch. I'd like to see you after we graduate." He'd said, but never acted on those words.

She'd seen him exactly three times between high school graduation and her twenty-fifth birthday. The first two times, she'd shocked him again. He'd not recognized the sophisticated lady shopping at the local grocery store to help her mom get provisions for Thanksgiving dinner. He'd stammered and said "Hi". The second time, she was having coffee with her gal-pals at the local diner on a Valentine's Day when they were celebrating their pending college graduation. The third and final time was on his birthday when Geneva was buying a birthday cake for her grandma at the local bakery. She'd met Tony and his younger brother Martin picking up his "quarter-century" cake for the huge family party planned the next day.

Martin had always been her pal and he was the only member of Tony's family that had known about Geneva's case on his brother. He looked at her and his brother and did his classic "wingman" best to leave them alone together. He'd taken Geneva's cake to her car and placed it safely on the back seat then he'd told Tony, "Hey man, I got the cake. How about you and Gene catch up." He'd not waited for an answer, but shooed them out the door.

Tony had started it, "Good to see you."

"Good to see you too."

"You look good."

"You look great; that's a great haircut."

Back and forth they'd started with small talk. They'd ended up with her meeting him for a late coffee date after her Grandma's party. They'd sat in his truck talking for a couple of hours. He'd driven her to the mountain overlook where all the kids had "necked" in high school. They'd talked about that. He'd admitted to taking a date there once or twice. She'd admitted that she'd never been there with a boyfriend.

The talking moved onto kissing of course. The kissing was electric. Her hair came down. His jacket came off. Soon enough they were both half-naked and too hot for the car. Geneva became overwhelmed. It was like all her teenage fantasies had merged into this crazy make-out session. She cut it off. "I'm too old to get naked in a car. I have an apartment for Pete's sake." She'd exclaimed as she'd torn herself away. She tried to get her top back in place as she asked, "Take me home, please. I can't do this."

Tony's answer was like a bucket of ice water. "I shouldn't be doing this either. I don't know what I was thinking. I'm engaged to be married next month."

The uncomfortable car ride home stayed with Geneva a long time. It was a hell of a way to celebrate his birthday. Later she'd verified the wedding details with her buddies in town. She'd also found out that Tony had planned on telling his family about the engagement that same night. Martin had gotten royally pissed at his brother for holding that back. He'd called Geneva to apologize and admitted that he'd not have put them together had he known that his "good for nothing ass" of a brother was already engaged.

Geneva had learned about Rosemarie Jones through the gossip and grapevines that are so prevalent in a small town. Rosemarie was the only child of a wealthy developer—the largest commercial builder in the state apparently. She was head over heels in love with Tony. They'd met at college and she'd blossomed once the engagement was announced.

Her daddy had bought them a big house on the hill. Geneva's mom called her mousey. Geneva had wanted to hate her and think her ugly. But, then she'd met her at the engagement party. Rosemarie was sweet, and beautiful in an understated way. She had amazing golden eyes and true brown hair that was the color of rich wood. She moved gracefully and had a tinkling voice. Geneva was charmed by her. Geneva knew that they were just two different types of beauty. She'd left the party heartily depressed, but soon forced herself over it. Tony and she had never really hooked up. It was all fantasy anyway. "Well, she's welcome to him." Geneva told herself as she left the wedding party. She had done what she could to move on with her life. Not that anyone knew that her heart had cracked and healed that year.

On the outside all anybody saw was a girl who'd graduated college and moved back home to take over her family business. Her grandfather had started the auto body shop in the 1960's to help finance his car-craziness. Her dad had later run it with his brothers. Her dad was the oldest and the "heir." It was just too bad he'd only had daughters to inherit after him, so he'd handpicked his best nephews to take over with his eldest daughter Geneva. Geneva was the managing owner and ran the office as well as helped in the shop. Her twin cousins Joe and Bob aka Joseph and Robert, ran the shop proper. When necessary she could do her part and was usually the one called on to do the old-fashioned, curvy pin striping that required a steady hand and heart and an artist's eye. Geneva declared herself a success when on her twenty-seventh birthday they paid the final mortgage payment on the shop and she heard that Tony and Rosemarie had had their first baby, a boy, without flinching.

To celebrate buying the shop and to squelch her jealousy over Tony and Rosemarie, Geneva sold her fully restored 1979 Chevy truck and plunked down half the cash from the sale for a brand new crew cab. "Perfect for taking the boys AND my tools to town." She'd told her mom.

She had shut down the shop early that day to pack her gear into the new truck and to paint emerald green pinstripes down its black body. In a pair of her dad's old jeans and a faded red T-shirt, she'd braided her hair to keep it out of the way as she pulled the brush gently down the fender for the main stripe that would anchor the rest.

When she'd heard the bell over the side door, she'd called out, "We're closed. Come back tomorrow." without looking up as she finished the stroke. Each stripe was one stroke or none at all. She made it to the crack where the driver's door met the fender and lifted her brush when the customer called out. "Sorry to bug you, Gene. Do you have a minute?" It was Tony. He came over to her holding a bouquet of lilies. "Just wanted to give you these and tell you happy birthday."

He'd admitted he'd seen her mom at the bakery buying her birthday cake the day before. He'd been thinking that it was her birthday that day and he'd driven by and saw her everyday car—an old '67 Firebird—parked at the shop and had to stop.

Geneva later thought, *How do these things start? How does one start having an affair I wonder?* In her case, he'd stopped by the deserted shop unexpectedly. Seeing him in a private area started it, she supposed.

They'd talked for a couple of hours. He'd admitted to being lonely. Rosemarie had been in the hospital for the past month due to complications with her pregnancy. He'd said things like, "Don't get me wrong. I am so happy she and the baby are well. I've just been by myself in that big old house too much."

Geneva had known that the excuses were all flimsy. Tony wasn't as happy as he'd thought he'd be. Rosemarie was fixated on the baby. He was feeling neglected. Geneva knew he was being selfish. But, for the first time in her life, she was tempted, really tempted, even though she knew better than to mess with a married man. But, she also knew that Rosemarie was horribly sheltered and she could imagine how much intimacy they had NOT been sharing.

As they sat in her office, she looked at Tony and noted that he still looked handsome, but he looked tired and a bit forlorn like a lost puppy. She also knew he was doing it purposely. He'd always been this way as a young man. He'd act helpless so she'd bail him out of whatever mess he was in. While part of her was disappointed in him for not growing out of this, part of her was focusing on the chemistry around them. She couldn't deny that they had always had great chemistry—today was no different. And for once, it seemed that he was feeling it too. In the past, she'd always felt it, but he'd been clueless.

They'd started in the classic way—A night alone with no witnesses. They'd started by sitting next to each other on her Grandpa's old leather couch in the office just talking and relaxing. Somehow the lights got dimmed. Somehow they'd started touching. One thing led to another and Geneva experienced the best sex of her life. Geneva was no prude, but she'd also never had a real desire to fool around a lot. Her first experience had been as a freshman in college. After she and that boyfriend had split, she'd avoided men in general while she waited to find the spark.

She had the spark now. After, she'd shocked Tony by dragging him into the shop's tiny shower. He'd had no idea that the office not only had a couch and kitchenette, but full bath attached.

They'd cleaned up and when Tony had started to apologize and worry about Rosemarie, Geneva stopped him. She'd decided somewhere between the couch and the shower that she was going to not put too much effort into worrying about what they were doing. "Don't talk about her. This is between you and me and has its own rules. Don't talk about her with me, just like you won't talk about me to her. Go home to your wife and baby. I am fine right here." She'd meant it too. She was resolved to not expect anything from this thing between her and Tony but great sparks.

Somehow over the next few weeks, despite her determination to end it after just that one night, Geneva was unsuccessful in stopping the rendezvous. She *was* successful in keeping control of things. Geneva wondered where these mercenary tendencies to keep her life in check no matter the situation came from, but she couldn't deny them. Only her mom suspected she had a boyfriend. Her sisters and cousins were oblivious. Everyone stayed caught up in their own lives and respected her privacy, which only worked because no one had caught on. Geneva knew it couldn't last, but she was going to go for a record. Small towns might grow gossip like weeds, but some of the best damn secrets were also kept secret in a small town.

Geneva did what she could to protect Rosemarie, but she refused to live her life based on the needs of another woman. Tony met her on her terms when it was good for them. If Rosemarie needed him, Geneva had her own things to do and wasn't much bothered. She really made Tony's life easy.

After spending most of her life with a case on him, she found that she was highly adapted to live her life around an obsession with Tony with little disturbance of the status quo. She also refused to feel guilty about Rosemarie. Tony had started it. And, their history was nearly insurmountable sometimes. Besides, Rosemarie had the baby and had immersed herself fully in motherhood.

They went on for a year this way. Around the time Geneva heard that Rosemarie was pregnant again, she found out the same about herself. She'd gotten to know Tony very well by this time. She knew he was finally beginning to feel guilty. She knew how easy loving Rosemarie was to him and she had heard that she was a great mother. Tony started regretting being away every so often. *He no longer needs me.* Geneva thought, and realized that that thought didn't hurt.

She was finally over Tony. After more than a decade, she didn't love him anymore. It helped seeing how much he needed to grow a backbone or as Martin put it, "a pair of balls." What kind of man had no problem letting a girlfriend run his affair and a wife run the rest of his life?

Geneva felt differently too. She needed to be free instead of always watching what she said or did. The pregnancy changed her perspective. Oh, it was fine to screw around for just her, but it was no way to treat an innocent kid. This life was not good enough for her baby. Things gelled in Geneva's brain all of a sudden one day. She was about four months along. Rosemarie was five months. Geneva was reasonably sure she knew when Rosemarie's baby number two had been conceived and she decided that she was done with the affair. "Tony needs to become a man." She said to herself as she dialed the telephone to give Tony her news. He came over as asked.

"I can't believe Ron is moving us to California." Tony remarked.

"Your father-in-law wants the best for you and Rosemarie. I say just take the opportunity." Geneva replied.

"But, what about you, what about us?" Tony asked.

Geneva looked at him and knew his heart wasn't in it. *I am not going to tell him about our baby. I'll just break it off.* "Tony, there is no *us*, there never was. It's always been just two folks reveling in great chemistry. Go."

He went. She was glad. The body shop was settling down now that this quarter's jobs were finished, but it was the lull in the storm. Summertime meant big projects.

Tony and Rosemarie moved quick so that Rosemarie would be fully settled in the new home by her third trimester. Geneva pondered about what to do about her own impending "bundle of joy". She was pretty sure her mom knew she was pregnant. The weight gain was getting harder to hide, but the kicker was her swollen ankles. Her mom could tell by what boots she WASN'T wearing that something was off.

By her sixth month, Geneva was desperate. She needed a plan for the baby, NOW! Then inspiration struck her. She wasn't quite sure what to do with or after the pregnancy, but she knew who to talk to about the baby.

She'd called Rosemarie's dad Ron and asked him if he'd had a preference about what happened to *this* baby. She and Ron had developed a relationship of sorts. In fact, it was Geneva's fault that Tony and Rosemarie had to move. She'd called Ron months before, let him know about a few of Tony's extramarital activities, and told him to move his son in law away from his bad habits.

Ron liked her. They'd met when he'd found her business card in Tony's office. Tony had told his father-in-law that Geneva's shop had fixed his work truck after a wreck, which happened to be true. He'd liked the work and so Ron had brought in his '86 Corvette for a paint job and new seats. He and Geneva were die-hard GM fans and found common ground. They had hit it off immediately when he'd looked at her Firebird and remarked, "You need to trade that fire-chicken in for a real car, lady."

Geneva felt bad about having to break the second pending birth news to him. She liked Ron as much as his daughter. However, she wasn't that surprised when Ron admitted he *wasn't* surprised. He was a smart guy. It turned out Ron was relieved. Some of the guys on the crew had begun to suspect Tony was stepping out, and it was hurting morale. In their earlier conversation, Geneva told Ron that she'd meant no harm and that moving Tony out of state would be the best thing for him. Besides getting him away, the distance from family would hopefully help him man-up finally. Ron had agreed. Now he promised to support her with her baby. If she wanted to keep it or put it up for adoption, he would help her as needed.

Geneva looked at her life. At twenty-nine, she was certainly settled and capable of taking care of a baby. Then one night she dreamed of her dad. Even though he'd been gone for years, she dreamt of a long-ago Christmas with the six of them, her mom, dad, and sisters together at home. That dream decided it for her. Her baby needed a real family, not a cavalier, workaholic, single mom. She would give up the baby for adoption. Ron knew a couple of folks. She'd call him and set things up.

★★★

"Tony, here's your mail." Rosemarie handed Tony a pile of envelopes on her way to the nursery. She was so happy. Their baby girl completed their family and Geneva's little girl would have a good home too. She was glad that her dad and Geneva had found a good family for Tony's other daughter. *I'll have to take Geneva to lunch one of these days when I'm back visiting the old hometown. We've both had a chunk of a good man with bad habits.*

Rosemarie was glad of Geneva's honesty. She'd agreed to let Ron talk to Rosemarie about her and Tony and the baby. Ron had told Rosemarie what Geneva had said about Tony. Rosemarie was glad that Geneva knew her husband well enough to know the only thing that would make him a better husband was distance—distance from his past, crutches, and bad habits. She was grateful that Geneva had shared the truth about the situation with her dad. The move away from everything he knew helped Tony be less insecure, because it was "do or die" in his mind. Then he became more focused on her and the kids. Finally after four years of marriage they were finally a family.

Diapering finished; Rosemarie came back into the kitchen. She heard Tony dial the phone and smiled. She looked at the birth announcement in her hand. Annabelle Rosemarie was born last week and her proud, adoptive parents were grateful that God had found a way to provide them their own little angel after years of waiting. At the bottom of the collage of baby pictures she saw Geneva's handwritten message and smiled as she read it, "I am glad he came back to you. I can never make up for what I did. But, I am sorry. I hope changing my phone numbers puts the final nails in the coffin. Be safe and happy."

Rosemarie heard her husband curse and stomp into his office. *No doubt looking for her cell phone number.* She thought as she twirled Geneva's new business card in her hand. "I wonder if I should ask him about her?" She chuckled and tucked the card and announcement into her purse. "Nah. Let him stew."

6

Her Babies Too

Amelia looked down at the little faces below her. The two little boys looked so precious to her. Their father had bundled them in their matching parkas and left them standing by the front door while he ran out to start the SUV. She faltered in zipping up her coat as she took in their expressions. Little Matthew was staring up at her expectantly. She could tell he was scared. His two-year-old eyes looked up her with such trust. He stood totally still braced to "stay" until she or his daddy would return. Michael meanwhile had sat down and was looking bored. She'd told them to wait for her "just a sec." while she'd ran upstairs to grab her scarf. There was Matthew exactly where she'd left him. She'd zipped him up and tightened the tie on his hood and placed his little fuzzy blanket in his arms. He stood there holding it in the exact same position. Her heart wrenched. This little person, so new to this world had trusted her to return. His trust was implicit. She felt a deep guilt. She'd lingered upstairs. Her main worry was whether to wear the silvery blue scarf that brought out the color of her eyes, or the red one that went so well with her coat. Such trifles, and her wavering caused her to delay overlong. Meanwhile, these two little boys had waited for her.

All the worries and stress in their lives and she couldn't even keep them foremost in her thoughts at times.

Tears came to her eyes as she knelt down to hug the little ones. Matthew's relief radiated from him as he hugged her back tightly. She pulled Michael into the hug. He held his nearly five-year old body stiffly at first, but then relaxed and joined the hug. These two were precious to her. She loved them as much as if they were her very own. She forced the lump in her throat back down as she thought of their father. She loved them for themselves, but that love had deepened with the love she had for their father.

Over time, she'd realized he seemed uptight because of the strain he was under. Brandon was fighting the chaos in his life by maintaining rigid control over himself and his boys. Later she'd got to know him better. Once they'd found a routine and rhythm, he'd begun relaxing around her and they'd become friends. Amelia just hoped that he still thought of her as a friend and an employee, because she'd fallen in love with him months ago.

She and Brandon were leaving today for the first trip of many until things were settled. Brandon would be moving with his sons to Idaho Falls to be nearer to their mother. Their mom Janice was out of rehab and on probation.

Soon, he wouldn't need full-time childcare anymore. Amelia's heart was broken. Brandon had needed her, really needed her once. He'd spent the last eighteen months grateful for her help. But, she was just a helper to him. When she'd heard the good news about the boys' mom, she'd evaluated her life. She was determined to move on. He would be moving on, so she needed to too.

Amelia sighed, *He can't even see me as a woman. Just a friend or 'the nanny.'* She thought as she released the boys. Hefting Matthew to her hip and transferring the blanket to his mittened hands wasn't an awkward move anymore. Michael waited for her to reach down and grab his hand with her free one. He was just large enough to open the front door. Together the three of them moved outside as a unit.

The bitter cold engulfed them on the porch. January was always the coldest month up here. The snow from Christmas ten days before was still around, but the wind had sculpted the Utah powder into ice-crusted drifts and slick layers on the concrete sidewalk. The temperature was hovering in the low teens.

She could see Brandon had started his Chevrolet Tahoe and was scraping frost off the windows. The exhaust visibly steamed white vapor into the bitterly cold air. Thankfully the wind had ceased, but the sun had set, and the night would be cold. She watched the muscles move across Brandon's back and shoulders as he stretched and reached with the scraper to clear the passenger windows. He moved to the back window as she arrived at the SUV. She opened the rear passenger door and boosted Michael in where he squeezed past his brother's car seat to his booster seat on the far side.

Matthew shifted from her arm to his seat comfortably. He waited patiently for Amelia to tuck his "wubbie" blanket around his sides and then tuck it in around his legs after she buckled the straps. He smiled back at her as she reached up to the rear-compartment heater to make sure warm air was circulating in the back seat properly. Michael had reached his seat and instead of waiting patiently for her, he leaned over and grabbed for her scarf. Michael had grown fond of her perfume and liked to play with her scarves lately rubbing them against his nose. Quietly laughing she bent down to let him unwind it from her neck. She thought, *I'm glad Mom let me use the soft silvery yarn we found at the Needlepoint Joint last year to make that scarf. Anything else, and I'd have a rug burn on my neck from that kid.* She said, "Okay, Mike, I'm coming over to do your seatbelt. Wait for me."

Patting Matthew to reassure him that he would be okay, Amelia backed out of the SUV and shut the door. She shivered and was glad the SUV had warmed enough for the heater to push out warm air towards the boys in the back seats. She quickly moved around the back of the SUV to reach the passenger door. Brandon was working on the driver's window and moved on to the mirror when he saw her approach.

★★★

Whenever Brandon saw Amelia he was amazed at her. The brown curls of her hair amazed him, with its many colors. The silver of her gray eyes amazed him, because her irises were so light compared to her dark lashes. Right now, with her skin pale in spots and red and chilled in others, her eyes really stood out. The inky black eyelashes she'd inherited from her mom framed eyes that showed her every thought. Her hair was down today "to keep her ears warm" in her words, and the curls stood out and away from her head and hung over her shoulders as if to defy the freezing air from pressing them down. She glanced at him and smiled as she opened the passenger door in her usual efficient manner. He watched her buckle up his oldest son. She carefully wrapped her scarf securely around Michael's neck and helped him arrange the ends just so and patted his hands and smiled. He'd watched her nestle his younger son in his wubbie with as much care. Brandon made a show of clearing the last of the frost from the windshield as she went around the back of the SUV to get to the front seat. *She won't even walk by me.* He thought. Amelia continued in her usual tasks to help him with the boys, but she'd forced distance between herself and him, as their daddy. She remained as professional as possible, but he could tell already, though they hadn't finished discussing it, that his moving away would end their relationship.

Brandon sighed. He had no choice but to move. Janice, his ex, had convinced everyone that she could stay clean this time, but she needed to do it in Idaho Falls near her family. Tonight was a test run. If it went well, Brandon had three months to sell out in Utah and find a house within twenty-five miles of his ex in-laws' house. Brandon prayed silently as he got in the driver seat, "Please, Lord, let it work this time, or let this be the last time I have to fight with Janice for the boys."

***

The ten-minute ride to the freeway was uneventful. Amelia sat quietly as did the boys as they drove. Brandon hadn't spoken, and she didn't know what to say. She was relieved to hear little Matthew state the obvious when Brandon pulled off the highway, "We going to get gas?"

She answered, "Yes, baby. Your daddy has to gas the Tahoe so we can make it to Idaho Falls to your momma and grandma."

Matthew's response was typical, "Bug juice?"

Michael chimed in at this point, "Yeah, can I get one too?"

Amelia caught Brandon's eye so she could see whether he disagreed with her proposal as she gave it to the boys. "Yes, but I need to go get them for you. It's too cold out there for you guys to go into the station with me." Brandon gave a small nod, so she continued, "So, we'll wait here until your daddy's got the gas, and then I'll go in and get us some drinks, okay."

Two little voices said, "Okay."

Brandon motioned to the glove box, "Can you get me the notebook?"

"Sure, but I can write down your mileage if you like."

"Okay. Go for it."

Amelia grabbed the notebook, and then shuffled past the insurance, registration, and service papers to get the "space pen" Brandon liked to use in the SUV, because it worked in the bitter cold. He read out the mileage from the odometer and then got out to start pumping the gas.

Amelia wrote down the date and mileage and noticed the many entries in the notebook. Brandon liked to keep a record of his gas mileage each tank and periodically used them to measure his fuel performance. She noticed that of all the tanks on this page, representing about three months of fill-ups, half the entries were in her handwriting and the rest were in Brandon's. She couldn't keep herself from admiring his clear and confident writing. She looked over her shoulder to where he stood stoically letting the wind blow around him as gas pumped out of the nozzle. He happened to look over at her at that same moment and saw her looking at him. He smiled and Amelia smiled back and then looked back to the front of the SUV.

Soon enough they pulled out onto I-15 heading north. Amelia looked back to ensure Michael and Matthew were handling their Bug Juices well before turning to Brandon, "I got you a liter of Coke. Do you want it now?"

"No, I'm okay for now."

Amelia turned back to face forward to watch the lights in the dark night. She thought about the latest development between Brandon and Janice. They had only been married for six months when Brandon found out about Janice's dependency problems. Janice had just found out she was pregnant and Brandon found her drinking one night. He'd told her Janice had gone on a bender when she'd found out she was pregnant. Brandon had known Janice had been drinking and smoking since she was about fifteen, but had thought she'd stopped before they'd gotten married. Getting pregnant for the first time scared her and she fell back into the bottle. Amelia sat quietly remembering the whole sad tale. *It's going to be a long ride up to Idaho Falls.*

Brandon had worked hard with his parents and Janice's to keep her sober through her pregnancy with Michael. She actually made it through the second half of the pregnancy sober and seemed to blossom into motherhood. For the first few months after Michael was born, she was happy and seemed delighted to be a mom, and Brandon thought the drinking was over. Then, she got pregnant again. Brandon wouldn't talk about that time, but Brandon's mom had told Amelia that Janice had gotten pregnant even though they were using condoms and neither was happy to find out they were pregnant again.

The second pregnancy with Matthew was worse for Janice. Brandon and the grandparents were able to keep her from drinking, but they couldn't stop Janice from smoking. When she delivered Matthew, Janice went into a deep depression. Amelia didn't meet the family until after, but she'd heard that Janice's depression went way past the "baby blues", and that eventually Brandon had feared for his sons' lives. It started when Janice would only take care of Michael and ignore little Matthew. Brandon did what he could and the grandmas started coming over to babysit and stay with the boys as much as possible.

Then one night Brandon came home after bedtime and found that while Michael was tucked in, Janice had left Matthew on the living room floor in a dirty onesie on a blanket. He must have been crying for hours, because by the time Brandon came home, the little guy was too hoarse to cry. He didn't look good, but stopped crying and started hiccupping when his dad picked him up. Brandon held him tight as he rushed through the house. He couldn't find Janice anywhere. Her car was in the drive, but he couldn't find her in the house. He hurried back into the nursery and changed Matthew's diaper. The diaper was more than full, and the plastic outer coating was barely holding everything in. The poor little tyke's bottom was red and irritated from being in a soiled mess for so long. Once he had him cleaned up with ointment on the worst bits, Brandon went into the kitchen to find some formula.

He was holding the bottle for Matthew's greedy sucking when he heard a car pull in and out of the drive. The motion sensor turned on the porch light and he heard keys jangle against the lock. He sat holding Matthew and trying to stay calm as Janice finally got the front door unlocked. She stumbled in, disheveled with her shirt and bra-strap falling off one shoulder and her hair in her face.

She didn't notice Brandon as she stumbled past him on the couch to the kitchen. He heard her drop her keys and purse on the table and then make her way to their bedroom. After a few minutes he heard the bed creak and her start to snore.

By then Matthew was full and tuckered out. Brandon placed him gently in his crib for the night as he went to check on Janice. Slathered on makeup was smudged across her face and pillow. Her hair was ratted and sticking up in weird ways. She'd dropped her clothes on the floor by her bed and he could smell stale cigarette smoke and cheap whiskey all over her. Fighting back his temper, Brandon went back into the kitchen to rifle her purse. He found matchbooks from Janice's favorite bar, receipts for liquor, and then some tiny balloons in the bottom of the purse.

He never found her syringes or could figure out when and where Janice shot up the heroin, but that was the last straw. When an intervention didn't work, Brandon had her committed for a three-day suicide watch to see if he could get Janice to snap out of her destructive cycle.

Then at his four-month check up, Matthew tested positive for opiates. An investigation showed that Janice had given the baby whiskey to sooth his gums as he was teething, and when he wouldn't shut up, she'd put a tiny amount of heroin powder on his tongue to make him quiet.

That was Brandon's last straw. He filed child abuse charges against Janice and told her to get out, go into rehab, and clean up or divorce him. She chose the drugs over him. Then, mid-way through the divorce, she got picked up for pushing drugs and got two years for drug possession with intention to distribute.

Brandon packed up his boys and moved out of state the week Janice was sentenced. Only after she was paroled did she even consider the terms of their divorce or the custody of the boys. In the years since, Brandon retained full custody and Janice was granted periodic visitation. Something usually went wrong around her visiting times, and she'd back out of the visits at the last minute, but harangue him over the phone later.

Amelia'd heard that Janice tried to be polite when she'd called over the holidays. She said she wanted to see the boys over Christmas when she'd called Brandon on Thanksgiving. Then she'd missed a meeting with her probation officer and had to serve thirty days in jail. Now that she was out of jail again, she'd asked that Brandon let the boys stay with her and her parents in Idaho Falls for a few weeks.

When Brandon told Amelia about this latest visit, he also told her the judge's latest custody terms. He explained that he must move the boys closer to their mother so she could more easily visit with them. Brandon was reluctant, but his mother convinced him to allow Janice another chance. Amelia also knew that Brandon felt guilty that he hoped it would be her last chance; that this visit would convince Janice to give up her parental rights. *I don't think he believes she can ever live sober.*

Amelia met Brandon and the boys during her job interview to be their first live-in nanny/housekeeper. Her mother worked with Brandon's mother years ago and brought her his ad. Amelia had finished her bachelor degree, but wanted to take a year off or so before starting law school. She was considering being a nanny just because it was so different than then her job being a technical writer for a large manufacturing firm that had put her through college.

Brandon's mom was a good ten years older than her mom, so Amelia had imagined Brandon as a forty-something with two kids, not the twenty-six-year-old that greeted her for her interview. He was much closer to her age of twenty-four than she'd hoped. She wasn't worried about being attracted to him, as he'd struck her as a perfectionist and a snob when she'd first met him. But, she'd been charmed by Matthew and Michael, and they were taken with her, so she'd taken the job. Brandon agreed to give her a five-day workweek trial starting Monday. If she worked out well for them, he'd decide whether to give her the contract that following Saturday. She'd been happy to care for the boys and the house for more than a year now.

★★★

Brandon checked the rear-view mirror, and saw that Matthew had fallen asleep. Michael's face was lit by his hand-held video game. Amelia had given him *Mario Cart* for Christmas and he was quickly learning to master the game. He looked over to Amelia; she was resting her head against the seat's headrest looking out the window. He figured she must be thinking about something, because now that it was fully dark, there was little to see along the freeway but some far away house lights. He thought about the significance of this trip. If Janice was finally sober, she could take back some of her motherly duties. She could help him raise the boys.

Brandon considered Amelia's position in a world that included the boys' mother having regular custody. He would love to keep Amelia on full-time regardless of Janice's involvement. *Maybe this change will lessen her load, so she can take more time off.* For the past year plus, he'd tried to give Amelia a day off each week, and he let her take off anytime that the boys were with his parents or Janice's parents. But, that was her only time off from her nanny/housekeeper duties.

Brandon thought back to the first week Amelia had worked for them. He'd said five days, but by Tuesday or Day Two, he was glad to sign Amelia's yearly contract. In those two days she'd cleaned his whole house, found a way to get finicky Michael to eat something at every meal, and had helped Matthew be able to sleep in his own room for the first time in months. He was convinced Amelia was a keeper.

After three months, she was an indispensable member of the family. Brandon found himself looking forward to the lunches she made for him for work. He didn't know how she could handle being at his and his boys' beck and call twenty-four/seven unless a grandparent was around. *I wish she'd talk this over with me one more time, so I can get a read on her feelings about this change.* Brandon checked the mirror. Michael was now sleeping. Now that both boys were asleep they could talk.

"Hey, Amelia, you asleep?"

She laughed quietly, "No, just resting. What's up?" She automatically looked behind her to ensure the boys were okay.

"I haven't had a chance to really talk to you about Janice lately, and since the boys are finally down, I figure now is a good time." He glanced over at her and she nodded, so Brandon went back to watching the road as he talked. "Her mom believes she's turned a corner. She said she's been consistent taking her methadone, and has started taking some workforce training."

Brandon saw a road sign announcing they were only a half-hour out of Idaho Falls, and started to feel anxious as he continued, "She said that Janice only missed the appointment with her probation officer, because she'd taken a bus across town to her shrink and couldn't make it back in time. I'm not sure I believe that, but I'm going to give her the benefit of the doubt for now."

"Well, it's good that she's coming back to a more stable lifestyle isn't it?"

"Yes. We had such hopes. I always figured Janice would be a successful veterinarian. But, when I said we should wait to get married so she could go to school, she declined and said she'd rather be a stay-at-home-mom. I guess that plan worked until we learned that she couldn't handle pregnancy real well." Brandon looked over to Amelia and shrugged.

She cocked her head, "Well. I have to give her some credit. Taking care of an infant and a toddler at the same time is hard work. And, if she was in the midst of the baby blues, and couldn't see a way out, I can see how things could get overwhelming."

Brandon peeked over and saw that Amelia was looking out the window again as she finished speaking. He could always tell when she figured he wouldn't like what she was saying, because she'd look away from him. He said, "Well. I couldn't see it. And, while I try to understand it, I just can't. You didn't see how bad the boys were, and I didn't know what to do." He paused, not wanting to offend her, "But I'll try to dial back my anger at Janice. Mom said she is trying. And, I am driving up to hand over my boys for weeks, preparatory to changing up my entire life for her visitation."

That got Amelia's attention and she turned back to him. "You're right. She did do some pretty awful stuff, so it would be hard to trust her. I'll support you in whatever you decide. You know that I have nothing to do until the spring but help you pack and move." She smiled.

Brandon frowned thinking of Amelia leaving him in April. Her year contract expired, but she'd promised to stay until sometime in April. After that she was headed to California. She had an uncle who was a tax attorney and professor at Stanford. His clerk was getting married and so he would have an opening. Amelia could clerk for him and learn how to be a paralegal. He wanted her out there after tax season. Then, if she liked it, her uncle would support her getting her law degree from Stanford and becoming a partner in his firm. So, whether or not he and Janice found a way to share custody, he'd have to find a new nanny and maybe a housekeeper too in just a few months. He ignored the thought that slipped into his head, *Why am I more worried about losing Amelia than I am over having to move?*

Brandon consciously pushed his worries about losing Amelia, finding a new nanny, or a new house out of his head as he approached the freeway exit closest to Janice's parents' house. It was nearly nine PM and he hoped the boys could handle the stress of sleeping in a strange house tonight and then survive being reunited with their mother for the first time in a year.

He pulled into the driveway and parked. He spoke softly to Amelia, "She must have been watching for us." as Janice opened the door and came outside. Brandon and Amelia opened their doors in sync to get the boys.

Janice looked pale, but calm, calmer than he'd seen her since she'd first had Michael. She looked thinner, and she'd cut her hair, but the wild look was gone from her eyes. She seemed genuinely happy to see Matthew and gave a sweet smile to Amelia as she took him from her arms. Brandon was shocked that Matthew went to Janice docilely. He held himself quietly and looked his ex in the eyes.

Finally Matthew spoke, "'Melia says you're the princess."

Before Brandon or Janice could ask Amelia what Matthew meant, Michael spoke, "Matty!" You're not supposed to tell her about that."

Janice asked, "About what?" She looked to Brandon and then Amelia when Brandon shrugged. Amelia turned pink, but forged through her embarrassment as was her habit to explain, "I told the boys that you were the princess of a far away kingdom, and wanted to be with them, but an evil dragon had carried you away. And, that you would come back when you had finally defeated him. They've been waiting for you to come back." Amelia looked down and smiled at Michael to reassure him, as she provided the adult footnote to her explanation, "Michael heard Brandon speaking to your mom, and when she said that you were 'coming back to yourself,' he didn't know what that meant." She addressed Michael as she finished, "I told him that "coming back to yourself," means coming home after a dark and scary journey. While you were away, you were so scared that you didn't feel like yourself, and so when you made it back home safe, you finally felt more like your old self." Amelia looked Janice in the eye. "Sorry if my explanation to him wasn't right."

Janice smiled and blinked away tears, "No. That sounds exactly right." Janice looked first at Matthew as she smoothed the hair back on his forehead, then she looked down at Michael, "You were exactly right. A big dragon did take me away, and I fought him off. He may come back for me one day, so I have to stay strong and be ready to fight him off. In the meantime, I'd like to spend some time with my boys. You are my treasures, and I am glad I could make it back safe and get home to you." Michael ran over to her and hugged her legs as she reached down to hug him with her free hand.

Brandon figured Amelia wanted to give them some family time when she gently nudged him and said, "I'll get the bags and take them into Janice's mom. Okay?"

He replied, "Sure go ahead. Tell them we'll be in in a minute."

Brandon watched Janice's mom greet Amelia and usher her into the house, then turned back to Janice. He was glad that Michael and Matthew seemed happy to see her. Amelia had told him that Michael had some memories of Janice, and she'd tried to keep them alive and happy by showing him their old photo albums. *Amelia's strategy seemed to have worked.*

He was happy to see Janice so happy to see her sons. She kept touching each one as if she wasn't sure they were real. All of a sudden Matthew yawned big and stretched, and before he could act, Janice was on it, like she'd been with Michael at that age, "Hey buddy. You seem tired, let's go in and say G'night to Grandma and Grandpa so you can go to sleep." Janice then consulted with Michael, "You okay going in right now?"

"Yes, Momma."

Janice smiled big when she heard his "momma" then her face looked sad as she looked up to Brandon. His heart clenched when she mouthed, "I'm Sorry."

He mouthed back. "No problem."

By ten PM Brandon and Amelia were back on the freeway on the way home to Utah. She spoke after he'd been driving a while, "You look tired. Do you want me to drive for a bit?"

"No, I'm good. I may let you drive when we get gas in Malad."

"Okay. I'm going to nap, then."

"Sounds good."

Brandon turned on some music and let it play quietly knowing it wouldn't disturb Amelia. He had a lot to think about. Tonight a huge weight was lifted off his heart. Janice was better. She *was* back, and would be okay. He had a good feeling watching her with the boys and with her parents. Her mom had told him they were doing everything they could do for Janice and were hopeful for the future. Seeing Janice with the boys made him believe her.

Janice's mom said she'd be most careful and watchful of them for the next two weeks. She said that if all went well, in May, when Janice would be off probation, Janice hoped to reconfigure her life and set up a new, more regular custody arrangement if she could find a job.

Janice and her parents had decided that she should stay with them. They had the room and the house even had a mother-in-law apartment downstairs so Janice could have privacy. Her other siblings all had homes and agreed that Janice could stay there as long as she liked and that she could help take care of her parents as much as they were taking care of her.

Brandon was glad of that housing arrangement. He knew that Janice did best with her parents. She'd rebelled and moved out of their house at fifteen. And, though she'd been staying with her grandmother at the time, she'd actually spent most of her time at her boyfriend's and his lifestyle had started her down her road to destruction. Later in high school, she'd moved back home and her parents helped her clean up and graduate.

Brandon realized he'd been subconsciously worried that the boys would fight being left with Janice, especially Matthew, who was just a baby when she'd left. He looked over to Amelia and thought, *Nope. Amelia had that covered too. Just like everything else, she had my boys' fears under control.* He smiled thinking of Amelia's dragon story. Amelia had told him she was convinced that the horrible things in fairy tales were there purposely, because kids encountered awful things in life, and they needed stories to help them learn how to survive those awful things.

I never thought I'd survive to see Janice back, or that I'd ever be able to leave the boys with her and have them be safe. Thank you, Lord, for your bounties, and please keep Janice well. Brandon was shocked at this feeling. He had been sure that Janice would overdose and die before she'd get sober. He wouldn't have bet for her or on her, but now he was glad that others had. He looked over to Amelia again. She was still sleeping. He knew that she'd say that he'd been taking care of his boys, which was just as important as Janice fixing her life.

Feeling hopeful for the future, he considered his plans. Ever since the night he'd learned Janice had gone back to drinking and was into drugs, he'd quit all long term planning. Then, one night after he planned tonight's trip, he'd had thoughts about whether he should get back together with Janice. Brandon shuddered. Everything in him screamed "NO" at that. Even if she stayed sober the rest of her life, he knew he could never trust Janice fully again, not with his heart. It was hard enough trusting her with his boys, and he was only able to do that, because she *was* their mom. *But, she was not as good as mom to them as Amelia has been.* That thought caught him by surprise.

Brandon was well aware of Amelia's ambition to be an attorney. She never spoke of "settling down" and having kids without prompting. She'd convinced him that this nanny thing was just a break from her law studies. It would tide her over until she was ready to be a mom—something she spoke of in far future terms if it came up. *Why do I care whether or not she takes off and becomes an attorney? All I really need is a good nanny for the boys. Amelia's been great, but it's time for her to move on.*

Just then, Brandon realized that he had the next three weeks off…really off. Janice had the boys, and he could really take off and go somewhere. His work had just finished a big contract, and the boss had given everyone an extra week of vacation. And, since Brandon hadn't taken his last two weeks vacation, his boss okayed him to take all three weeks now.

What I am going to do with myself? Thoughts of painting his house so it could sell faster or taking a cruise to the Caribbean ran through his head. For the first time in nearly five years, he was totally free of all obligations for the next few weeks. *What am I going to do? It's the middle of winter, so outside home or yard projects are off the table.* Amelia shifted and turned her face over towards him, distracting him by her movement catching his eye. He looked over at her in the dim green light from the dash. Her hair looked dark, and her skin was a minty green. Her lips were slightly parted as she slept and a curl had fallen over one eye. He realized for the first time looking at her across the way, that she was beautiful to him.

Thoughts of, *What am I going to do when Amelia leaves us, leaves me?* obliterated thoughts of what he was going to do for his time off. *What am I going to do for the rest of my life?* For the rest of the drive, he stewed and let his thoughts simmer. He let Amelia sleep through the gas pump stop at Malad, only waking her when he pulled into his home driveway.

He followed her into the house and upstairs. He watched her enter her bedroom and close the door, then he continued down the hall to his master suite. He lay in his bed that night wishing he knew what to do now that things were finally on the mend in his life.

Brandon came downstairs in his sweats the next morning, determined to have a lazy Sunday doing nothing but watching old movies on his Netflix. He was shocked to see Amelia downstairs, already dressed and ready for the day. She was talking on the phone. He heard "No, Mom. Sounds good. See you in an hour." Before she hung up.

He asked, "What's going on?"

Amelia jumped.

He must have scared her. *She must not have noticed me coming downstairs.*

She recovered and answered, "Oh, nothing much. I'm just going to Mom and Dad's for a week. I need to pack away some stuff there and decide what I'm taking to California."

"You're not going yet, right?" Brandon tried to keep his voice calm as he asked.

"No, no. Not 'til April, but my little sister wants my room now, so I need to clean it out. You know, box my stuff up and get it out for her."

"Okay. When are you leaving?"

"Oh, in about an hour. Mom is coming to pick me up." She left him sitting at the bar while she went back upstairs.

Brandon tried not to feel lost. *You can do this. You lived by yourself for two years while you finished school, after all. What's three weeks in your own house? Man up, buddy.*

He made it exactly three days.

★★★

"Ouch. Dammit, that hurt." Amelia exclaimed as she regained her balance and continued on her way to the garage with her last box. She'd slipped on an icy patch between the porch and the garage door and hit her hip against the porch column. Once she'd placed the box on top of the others, she considered her progress as she rubbed the sore spot on her hip. *Twelve full and clearly marked file boxes. Not bad for twenty-six years of life, I'd say.* Resolved to go in and clean a day's worth of dust and grime off in a warm shower, Amelia closed the garage door and was heading towards the house when her mom opened the front door and hollered, "Amelia, you have company coming."

"Where?"

"Up the road." Her mom answered as she pointed to the road.

Amelia looked to the end of her parent's two-mile long driveway from the highway and saw a dark SUV coming up. When it got closer she recognized Brandon's Tahoe.

Her mom had kept the door open and also watched him driving in for a second, then remarked, "Brandon called about three minutes ago saying he was on his way. I told him you were in the garage." With that she stepped back and closed the front door.

Amelia waited outside watching Brandon get closer. *At least I can cool off out here while I wait. Too bad cold air doesn't help dirt. I wonder why he's here. I hope the boys are okay.*

★★★

Brandon was glad he found her house. He'd dug up Amelia's parents' address from his files, having only come out here once before. He spotted Amelia standing on the driveway watching him pull in. *Good. There she is. Here we go.*

Brandon pulled up and was quickly out of the SUV. He rushed up to Amelia and stood staring at her drinking in her grungy sweatshirt and sweat-curled hair. She looked at him expectantly, "So, what's up? Are the boys okay?"

He smiled, feeling happiness flow through him now that he was with her again. "The boys are fine. Nothing much is happing, except that I'm not okay. I'm not fine. I found myself rattling around the house with nothing to do. At first, I thought it was due to the boys being gone. But that's only part of it. I'm not okay without *you*. I realized this morning, that my house, my life is utterly empty without *you*. I miss the boys, but my heart cries out for *you*. YOU CAN'T LEAVE ME. I can't take it. I can't be without you. Stay with me. Please stay with me." As he finished speaking he nervously ran his fingers through his hair and looked at Amelia waiting and hoping.

Her lips trembled, but she didn't speak.

Brandon didn't know what to say. He'd just declared himself, but she hadn't answered him. He decided to show her how he felt. Before she could move away, he moved in and caught him in his arms. Before she could move her head, he lowered his face and captured her mouth with a searing kiss. Soon their mouths were open and she was kissing him back. Kissing him back like she meant it.

He paused to say, "Oh God, Amelia, stay with me. Don't go to California; stay with me instead. Please stay with the boys and me. I need you." He kissed her again. He pulled back and looked at her. The animal male within him was gratified to see her lips were rosy and swollen from kissing him while his heart trembled in fear that she'd say "No". He met her eyes, which shone with unshed tears. "Well?"

"Oh my heavens, Brandon! Of course you rush in here out of the blue and try to spin my head. But it worked, I'll stay with you, but on one condition."

"What? You name it, and I'll give you anything."

"Marry me and give me a baby girl so I won't be so outnumbered in your house!"

He laughed, "That's two conditions, but I'll do my damndest to give you both!" and then they were kissing again, and that's how Amelia's mom found them a few minutes later.

7

Penrose is Perfect

"Penrose is perfect!" Jasmine exclaimed as she entered the grand old Victorian house. She turned back to her sister Melanie, "I am so glad Grandma left me this old place."

Melanie rolled her eyes and said sarcastically, "Yeah, right. You just can't wait to live in an old house in the middle of nowhere that's going to fall down around you in the next big storm." She pushed past Jasmine and huffed up the stairs with the two suitcases she'd brought from the car for her.

Jasmine stuck her tongue out at her sister's back and wheeled the cooler she'd brought in down the hallway past the stairs into the kitchen. After the hallway, the dark wood floors turned into classic marble tile in the sunny kitchen. Like the rest of the house, the kitchen had the high ceilings, tall windows, and intricate trim of most Victorian houses, but it had been updated sometime in the 1930s so it also boasted white subway tiles with black accent tiles. To her left was a screened door exiting to the garden area that matched another door on the right leading to the garage. Against the back wall stood the original cabinets with a large, split, porcelain sink centered under a massive window. The back of the house faced due west, so the late afternoon sun shone brightly into the kitchen making it feel whiter and brighter than it did at any other time of day. The old 1930s stove stood proudly to her right on the wall next to the door to the garage, while a 1980s almond-colored fridge loomed to her left in the corner where it sat squished into the void next to the last cabinet against the wall.

Grandma and Grandpa had lived in this house throughout all their sixty-five years of marriage. Jasmine approved of what they had done with it. She spoke out loud to herself, "Fixed what's busted, replaced what they had to, and made everything work together." Jasmine knew how to work with what she had, and decided that she didn't need to gut the kitchen after all. She liked it just like it was. She moved past the rectangular table that sat squarely in the middle of the room and wheeled the cooler to the fridge. Methodically she unloaded the perishables she'd brought from her parents' house.

Grandma had died a few weeks back, and while Grandpa was doing well mentally, his poor health required full-time nursing care. Jasmine and Melanie's parents had moved him into a new care facility when he'd agreed to honor Grandma's will which deeded the old home place to his youngest granddaughter. Jasmine made a sad smile when she pictured her grandpa. *He's not long for this world now that the cancer has spread to his lungs. I hope Grandma comes for him soon.* Grandpa had told his family that he no longer wanted to live in the old place now that his love had passed on. "I can't take care of it anyway. Better that Jasmine have it now so she can fix it up to sell or stay. I just don't care anymore."

Of their kids, all four had married and left Penrose years before. This meant all the grandkids had been raised far from the rural culture of Penrose, Utah. The kids had met together when Grandpa first got sick and had a family meeting about the old home place. None of the kids wanted to sell their homes and move back, so Grandma and Grandpa had met with each of their twenty-five grandkids. Jasmine was the only one even interested in the place. So without telling the family, the grandparents worked out their finances. They sold their car, moved to a twenty-four-hour assisted living center for seniors, deeded the house and farmland over to Grandma, as Grandpa was so sick no one expected him to live out the year, and then rewrote Grandma's will to lay out everyone's inheritance.

When Grandma had died unexpectedly from complications of pneumonia just a month after living in the care home, the family was devastated. Then her will stunned them. Following it, the family lawyer sold the farmland to a neighbor in Penrose, deeded the house and the acre it sat on to Jasmine, set half of the proceeds from the land sale aside for Grandpa's care, and cut everyone else a check. When some of the heirs questioned the value of the house in comparison to the checks given to other grandkids, the lawyer squelched all complaints and demonstrated the strength of the will.

Jasmine scowled when she pictured one of her aunt's sour expressions during their confrontation. *Damn it. She didn't have to be so nasty. I guess money does trump blood.* Jasmine was grateful that her grandfather and parents supported her against the complainers. *They'd shut up if they knew what it will cost to keep this old place going, let alone the heating and other utility bills.* Melanie's arrival downstairs broke Jasmine out of her thoughts.

"Whew. It's hot up there. I'd tell you to get air conditioning, but then you'd have to buy a new furnace, redo all the HVAC, and insulate this sad pile of bricks. Good riddance to you."

Jasmine fought to stay positive in the face of her sister's bad attitude. "Thanks for taking my bags up, Mel. I plan to look into insulation options when I have Ben look over the bricks. If we have to parge the entire house, it won't be too much trouble to add more insulation after we gut all the walls."

"Better you than me. I'd have that Ben character bring over his backhoe and knock this place down and start all over." Melanie came over and gave her a quick hug, clearly ready to go, "Gotta run. You got Grandpa's truck, so call me if you need me to bring up more stuff from Salt Lake."

"Okay. Love you."

"Love you too." And Melanie was out the door.

By the time Jasmine made it to the front door, Melanie had backed out of the driveway and was accelerating down the highway. Jasmine watched her car fade out of sight. "Yeah. Bye, sis. I wish you could understand my love of this place."

Jasmine went out to the garage to find Grandpa's old army cot. She plunked it down in the front room, which faced northeast and was the coolest room at this time of day. "I'll sleep here until I get the bedrooms done upstairs. I can use the sun coming in that window for my alarm clock." Janice told herself. She went back into the kitchen where she'd left her combination laptop case and purse sitting on the kitchen table. "Let's get a workstation set up and then we can plot how we're going to get this place up and going once again."

Jasmine plunked her bag down on the buffet table that was the only piece of furniture left in the old dining room besides an old floor lamp and now, the army cot. Grandma had emptied most of the house when she and Grandpa had moved to the care center. Jasmine and Melanie's mom with her siblings had cleaned out what remained after her death. Jasmine went through the house and mentally inventoried the remaining furnishings.

1. *Dining room: Built-in china hutch, buffet table with splintered leg repair, 1890's floor lamp converted to electricity in the 1920s.*
2. *Kitchen: Appliances, cabinets, and sturdy, but ugly oak kitchen table with two chairs that don't match it or each other.*
3. *Hallway and downstairs powder room: ancient Kirby vacuum, old straw broom, bucket with a few cleaning rags and chemicals, over the toilet bookstand, dead plant in planter.*

4.   *Upstairs: four mostly-empty empty bedrooms plus bathroom.*

    a.   *One master bedroom with old steel bedframe that maybe fits a double bed, old apple crate for a nightstand, Space Bags full of linens*

    b.   *One bedroom that is empty but for a Space Bag holding two pillows*

    c.   *Another bedroom that's totally empty*

    d.   *Smallest bedroom has old sheets and a quilt in a box*

    e.   *Empty linen closet.*

    f.   *Bathroom with one towel, three rolls of TP, a bar of soap, and a toilet brush in stand. Only shower is here in the tub/shower combo*

"Okay, I'll sleep downstairs, but shower and dress upstairs." she decided as she went back downstairs.

Jasmine plugged in her laptop and Wi/Fi router. "Good thing I got the utilities and phone set up in my name today. Let's see how good the local DSL signal is." Her MacBook booted right up as the router showed strong DSL, Internet, and Wi/Fi signals. Shortly her computer indicated it'd found the network. Jasmine quickly connected to her email and checked her daily messages. "If only the family knew how well my software is doing, then they wouldn't worry about how much this place is going to cost to fix up."

Looking around, Jasmine felt satisfied in her current living conditions. She had a functioning bathroom, somewhere to sleep, somewhere to cook and eat, and somewhere to work on her computer to help pay the bills. "This will do nicely. I have two months left of summer, so I should be fine so long as we get this place fixed up by then. Time to demo."

★★★

Ben Cruise inventoried his to-do list for the remainder of his day as he pumped diesel into his work truck. His dad and younger brother were heading out to Soda Springs, Idaho to start the brickwork on a new elementary school. That job would keep the family well fed, but would take the entire crew and the rest of this month to finish. In the meantime, Ben's dad had asked him to stay at home in Penrose to help Old Man Nelson's granddaughter fix up the old Nelson house. Ben shook his head. Before Ed Nelson had gotten so sick, he'd asked Ben's dad to look over the old Victorian's brickwork and give him the full story on what it'd take to fix it.

Ben had worked with his dad to check out the bricks. The house was a two-brick wall construction from the 1890s. The bricks were mostly still strong, but the mortar needed redoing and some of the walls were pushed out due to the weight of the roof and the second storey.

Ben's dad was honest in the report: Redo ALL the mortar, add star brackets and bars to hold the walls in at least two points on each wall, and gut the insides so they could parge ALL of the brickwork on the inside. Grandpa Nelson had agreed that that would be doable, as he was planning on gutting the place eventually. The old plaster walls were mostly patches, and though he'd upgraded the plumbing in the 1960s, he needed to upgrade the electrical from it's current hodge-podge that would make an inspector cry.

Supposedly, starting tomorrow, while Ben's dad and crew began the cinderblock construction of the school, he was supposed to go help the Nelson granddaughter get started gutting her grandparents' place, and then over the next few weeks, work on the bricks to keep the old grand Victorian standing for another one-hundred and twenty years.

Once the pump clicked to indicate the tank was full, Ben replaced the nozzle and pocketed the receipt. *I'll call Miguel about a new roof next week.* he thought. His good buddy Miguel remodeled houses for a living, and had some free time this week while he waited for his most recent project's footings to set. Miguel was a whiz at roof repairs and had a crew capable of scaling the nearly forty-five-degree angles of the Nelson Victorian roof. *I hope the granddaughter can afford a good metal roof this time. Some of the worst damage to the bricks was due to near-constant roof leaks and a bad down spout.*

As Ben pulled up to the road, he saw an old blue pickup coming near to pass in front of him. As it passed, he saw the truck had a white stripe, red shell, and a brunette girl driving it. "That's Old Man Nelson's truck. No one else has a truck that old, that color, with that mismatched shell." When he saw the old black on white letters license plate, Ben was sure. "I bet that's the granddaughter." Following an impulse Ben turned left instead of right and followed the truck.

★★★

Jasmine pulled into Tremonton, Utah proper after she crossed where I-84 cut through the west side of town. She was heading to the lumberyard to get supplies and the new doors for the house. She'd found Grandpa's old sledge hammer, but needed a crowbar or a heavy pry bar to help her pull down the lath and plaster wood strips from the walls. The lumberyard had called because her new, custom, solid-wood front and back doors had arrived, so she'd figured she'd pick up some other demo supplies while she was in town. *The lumberyard closes at five, but the hardware store is open 'til nine. I better get the doors first.*

★★★

Ben pulled into the lumberyard right after the Nelson truck parked and the girl got out. Ben took note of the curvy shape, long legs, and long hair, as he followed her into the building. He made it up behind her as she announced, "I'm here to pick up some doors. They're for the Nelson place out in Penrose." She handed the lumberyard clerk her receipt.

Kypp, an old high-school buddy of Ben's who ran the lumber yard with his aunt, was working the counter and Ben heard him answer, "Yup. We got them in this morning. Let me go check on them and then I'll bring them out to you. Just a sec."

Then Kypp looked past the girl to Ben, seemingly prepared to help him too before he went in the back, "Hey Ben. What can I do you for?"

"Nothing right now, Kypp." Ben gestured to the brunette girl who'd looked over her shoulder at him, and pointed, "I'm helping Old Man Nelson's granddaughter redo the old place."

Kypp nodded and said, "Okay. Be right back."

As Kypp left for the stock room, Ben stepped up to the brunette and held out his right hand, "Nice to meet you. I'm Ben Cruise. I was in town and spotted you driving the Nelson beast, and figured I'd introduce myself. I take it you're the granddaughter?"

The brunette smiled back at him and shook his hand as she answered, "Yes. That's me. Jasmine Sims, granddaughter to Minnie and Edward Nelson. I take it you're the Ben Grandpa told me would be fixing my bricks?"

Ben flashed his best smile as he took in her brown eyes, "You got it. Did I hear that you are picking up new doors today?"

"Yes. Grandma wanted a new wood door with a big glass window for the front and because it was a special order due to size and material, they ordered new back doors too." Jasmine looked sad for a minute as she continued, "It's too bad they didn't get in in time for Grandma to see them."

Ben couldn't help but offer some comfort, "I understand. At least she's in a better place now."

Jasmine smiled at him. "You're right, but I still miss her." To change the subject, she continued, "So Grandpa told me you could also help me with some of the demo and other work?"

"You got it. Besides the brickwork, he asked me to find someone to redo the roof and told me to help you do the reno work or get someone in to help you. I have some of my friends lined up, but I wanted to find out your plans before

I started anything. Depending on what you want, I can help you do the reno myself."

Before they could talk further Kypp returned and motioned Jasmine to follow him to the back, "Come back and ensure they'll work. Then I'll load them with the forklift. You have a truck right?"

"Yes." Both Jasmine and Ben answered and they all laughed.

Jasmine pulled out her phone and pulled up her electronic notes. Ben watched interestedly as she spelled out each door's measurements to Kypp who confirmed the size both with the invoice and a tape measure. Once they checked all the doors, Jasmine asked, "I pulled the truck in out front, do I need to back it in or pull it out back?"

Kypp answered, "No. That's fine. You can leave it there. I'll bring them out and pull behind you to load. There's plenty of room in the lot before you hit the road."

Ben followed Jasmine out to her truck. He watched her scrutinize his work truck as she walked past it to lower her truck's tailgate and raise the shell window. Then they both waited and watched Kypp pull the forklift behind the Nelson truck. Ben helped Kypp gently slide the three doors from the teeth of the forklift to the truck bed.

After Jasmine and Ben both thanked Kypp and he took the forklift back, Jasmine got to work securing her load.

When done, the nine-foot doors rested the full length of the bed and a foot or so past the lowered tailgate. Ben watched Jasmine fold a flap of the packing blanket padding the doors in the bed up and over the end of the doors to also pad them where the truck shell window would rest on them. She then used bungee ties to secure the shell window to the rear bumper against the top door. He reached to help her run a few more ties-downs to keep the doors from bouncing out the back of the truck. He smiled when Jasmine reached in her back pocket and pulled out a red bandana, which she tied to the top door to be the red "over-length load" flag.

Ben stood looking at Jasmine, wondering what he should say. She charmed him with her graceful, no-nonsense movements and the fact that she knew she had to flag the doors poking out the back of the truck. Clearly she was a woman who understood load rules of the highway.

Before he could speak, she spoke first. "So, Mr. Ben. I wanted to start demo-ing tonight once it cools down, and though I found a sledge and a pair of work gloves, I need a facemask, a bucket for nails, and crowbar for the lath strips. Do you want to follow me down to the hardware store, or head out to the house and take a look around?"

Ben squashed a distracting thought of this beautiful woman getting sweaty knocking down walls in the tiny t-shirt she was wearing, and cleared his throat so he could answer, "I have a big crowbar that's great for plaster at home, and a bucket and some facemasks for the dust here in the truck." He made a show of looking at his tough, but battered work watch, "If we head out now, we could get in three to four hours of demo by ten o'clock. Do you want to just head out to Penrose now?"

Jasmine looked surprised at his offer, but recovered quickly. "Sure. We could do that, but what about dinner? I have some stuff in the fridge for me, but don't you need to eat? Didn't you work today?"

Ben smiled, feeling pleased that she'd figured out that he was "after work". "Tell you what. How about I head home and get supplies and some dinner fixings, and then meet you at your Grandpa's in about forty-five minutes?"

"Sounds good." Jasmine stood looking like she wanted to say something else, but she must have thought better of it, because she reached out and took his hand, grasping it softly. "Thank you, Ben for helping me with this. You give me hope that I can really update Grandma and Grandpa's—that I can do this." She smiled and turned to get in her truck.

Ben watched her get settled then waved to her and moved to his truck. Jasmine motioned for him to go first, and reluctantly he agreed. He thought, *She'll probably take it easy on the drive home to save scratching those doors, and I need to get to my place and get some stuff. I better get moving.* as he pulled out. In his rear-view mirror, he watched Jasmine back out and slowly come down the road following him.

At the main highway, Ben turned west and considered what he'd learned over the past hour. Yesterday, he was just single guy working his fingers to the bone in the family masonry business he might own one day. Now, he was a single guy on a special assignment to help a beautiful girl update his idol's old house. Ben lost himself in fantasy thoughts about Jasmine as he drove home.

Grandpa Ed had told him that his granddaughter was the only one interested in the old home place. He'd said that if any of his sons or grandsons had wanted the farm, he'd have deeded it over to one of them. But, when only this one granddaughter had shown interest—and only interest for the house, Minnie and Ed decided to sell the farmland and deed the house over to her. All Ed had said about this granddaughter was that she worked for a computer company, so she could live anywhere, and that he'd hoped she find a nice guy and settle down somewhere to make him more great-grand babies and be happy.

Thinking back on that conversation, Ben wondered if Ed had been plotting something when he'd asked his dad whether *Ben* was free to work on the house. Ed knew perfectly well that while all the boys worked for the masonry business, Ben's brothers were all married. "I wonder if the old goat was match-making?" Ben asked himself, and then shock overcame him. "Hey. I don't care if he was. Jasmine is one pretty girl." Ben realized he could be working full-time along side Jasmine in her house for the next two months. On one hand, he was excited at the prospect. It'd be a great way to see if she was "the one" for him. On the other hand, she could be a hell of a distraction during a job that would surely turn ugly before it was over.

After about ten minutes, Ben reached Penrose and soon passed the Nelson house. He turned one more corner, and went down another quarter mile before he reached his house. He pulled into the driveway that his house shared with his childhood home where his mom and dad still lived. Since he'd turned twenty, quit college, and started working full time with his dad in the family business, Ben had rented his grandma's two-bedroom 1910 farmhouse from his parents. As he carried his work pack and lunch-kit into the kitchen, Ben couldn't help but think about Jasmine living all alone in the old Nelson house. Although he tried to not have it, the thought hit him, *I could marry her and move in there, and leave this place back to Mom and Dad. Wouldn't that be something?*

★★★

Jasmine sighed for the tenth time as she meandered Grandpa's old truck down the highway. Every so often she would look in the rear-view mirror to check the doors. Each time they were fine. All three were solid wood and very heavy. And, in between her worries that she would either hit a bump and bounce them out or turn to fast and have them slide out the truck, she couldn't stop thinking of Ben.

Jasmine couldn't help but notice Ben's tall height and meaty arms. He was taller than she'd expected. She also noticed how his blue eyes sparkled. He had very dark lashes and eyebrows, but very light eyes. She'd noticed they were a light color, but outside in the lumberyard parking lot she saw how blue they were. She'd also enjoyed how dirty Ben was. She had cousins that did construction for a living, and they got dirty, but Ben looked like he was covered in cement dust. It looked like his hair was as dark as hers, but his entire body from head to toe, had a gray coating, with splotches of lighter smears. Ben's face and back of his neck were clean, while the sides of his neck and arms were powdered. It looked to her like he'd swiped his face and the back of his neck with a wet rag, but not touched the rest. She smiled. She loved dirty men. She'd worked the past five years at the same software firm and was very tired of clean men who never set foot out of doors except for the journey from car to office and car to house. In her mind, Jasmine realized she equated clean with weakling. "So if dirty means manly, Ben is definitely a MAN." She giggled. She relished the feminine excitement she felt thinking about him. She spoke to herself as she took a deep breath, "I wonder if we'll have great chemistry?"

★★★

Ben checked his messages as he rifled his fridge. Because he was now equal-partners with his dad and brothers, his mom asked that he store the business phone over here to save her the hassle. Most days, he forwarded the landline to his cell phone, but today was the last day on their current house job, and he was way too busy to babysit the phone. Ben had spent the day going over all the brickwork with the owner, general contractor, and county inspector before helping his buddy finish pouring the house's concrete RV pad.

Ben listened to all six messages as he plopped two steaks, a head of lettuce and a couple of baking potatoes into an empty cooler. He grabbed a square of butter, the sour cream, and some of his mom's homemade ranch dressing from the fridge and placed it on top of the food and closed the cooler lid. Then he grabbed the message pad and captured the messages. Two were for him and those folks had called him on his cell phone too. One was from his dad telling him that the Nelson girl was in the house, and the other three were requesting new bids. Ben put those three in the pile for his youngest brother to handle and zipped the cooler out to the truck. He then opened his dad's garage and grabbed a couple of large crowbars, a smaller crowbar, and an empty five-gallon bucket, because the one in his truck was full of debris. Tossing those into the back of his truck, he got in and started to back out to the highway. He saw his mom. She'd come outside to her front porch and waved at him to stop, so he rolled down the window.

She yelled out, "Where're you going? Do you need dinner?"

"No, Mom. Thanks. The Nelson girl moved in today and I am heading over there to start some demo. We'll do dinner there, and I'll check in with you tomorrow."

"K, Son. Be safe. Love you."

"Love you too, Mom. I'll be in for breakfast with Dad tomorrow."

"K."

Ben smiled. He couldn't wait to get over to the Nelsons', and he didn't even care that his mom would interrogate him about Jasmine later. He had a good feeling about Jasmine. He liked her a lot already. Ben mused to himself. "Maybe I'll have her come over for breakfast. Mom misses cooking for all of us when we're on an outta-state job. She'd probably enjoy cooking for Jasmine and me while we fix Ed's house. Then Mom can give Jasmine the fifth-degree directly."

Jasmine's eyes lit up when she saw the steaks. Ben couldn't stop grinning when she commandeered the cooler and proceeded to pull out a roll of tinfoil so she could wrap the potatoes for baking. She looked at him and asked, "Do you care if I bake these instead of frying them?" She held up the steaks at him.

Ben shook his head, "Nope. Go ahead and cook them the way you like. I was going to cook them if you didn't want to."

"I like a man who lets me take charge. Especially today, when I am still figuring out what the aunts left in Grandma's cupboards." Jasmine answered as she turned away from him and started rummaging in the cupboard next to the sink.

Ben watched her scrutinize a tiny Dutch oven she found under the sink, then an ancient cast-iron frying pan. She scrunched her nose as she held the fry pan in one hand, and wiggled her fingers on her other hand as she stared at the stove. He decided both were unconscious "thinking" actions for her. All at once she decided, "Tinfoil dinners it is." Ben wasn't sure what she meant until he watched her get more tinfoil out. He watched fascinated as Jasmine plunked the steaks down on the tinfoil, and then rummaged in the fridge. She turned back and laid out oil, onions, celery, spices, a knife, the potatoes, and a cutting board on the counter. Then, she proceeded to pour some oil on the steaks, move them around on the foil to spread the oil. She then sprinkled a spice mixture that had a lot of coarsely ground black pepper on both sides of each steak. The vegetables were next. In short order, Jasmine rough chopped the veggies and threw them on top the steaks. Then she carefully folded the tinfoil into airtight packets folding the edges just so. When all her bundles were ready, she pulled out a steel half-sheet cake pan and placed the tinfoil bundles on it. The loaded pan went into the stove as she set the timer for seventy-five minutes.

When she was done, she turned back to Ben and announced, "I figure we can work for the next hour or so as these babies cook, and then take a break for dinner." Before Ben could reply, she'd moved past him and was up the stairs having grabbed a sledge, a facemask, and the five-gallon bucket on her way.

Ben looked around, "I think a hurricane just blew through here, but there's no proof." He'd known many a hard worker, and even some efficient ones, but he'd just watched Jasmine out-perform his best workers and even his mom. He noticed that she had even cleaned up her mess and placed the dirty items by the sink ready for the next wash. *If she demos like she cooks, we should make good time.* He thought as he trudged upstairs to follow her.

Ben and Jasmine worked out a system in short order. Ben was taller, so he took the top half of the walls. Jasmine was more flexible, so she took the bottom half of the walls. One would start on one side and work clockwise, while the other would start on the other side and move counter-clockwise.

As they worked they talked and Ben asked Jasmine about her life. He learned a lot. After only three years, she'd graduated college with honors with a computer engineering degree. She finished early because she'd taken only college and advanced-placement courses her senior year of high school. All of Jasmine's cousins were smart like her, but none of them had been headhunted by a large Silicon Valley software firm that was looking to open offices near Salt Lake City.

He asked, "What was it like? I mean I've never been headhunted at job fair."

She answered, "Well, it was really just like a job interview, only they asked me about working for them instead of the other way around. I was happy to take the job. I made a killer salary, but I wanted to save as much money as possible. I'd heard rumors that my new company was notorious for swapping out programmers and designers every few years. So, I bought a tiny house in an upcoming Salt Lake neighborhood from a bank auction. I lived there for three years working hard to renovate and restore it in my downtime. Meanwhile, I was a success at work and saved any bonuses I got."

He couldn't help but tease her, "And you're modest too."

She blushed. "I can't help it. I'm a damn good programmer. I was sure after four years, they'd swap me out for a younger model, but I ended up helping them land a lucrative contract for a huge engineering firm. My software was so successful and groundbreaking for them, that my bosses put it on the market for other engineering firms. They also gave me a direct share of the profits and offered me company stock with my annual bonus last year." Jasmine's voice turned sad, "Although, soon after that Grandpa got sick, and I felt I needed to reorganize my priorities."

"So what did you do? Did you quit after you made a killing on the software?"

"Not then, no. See, my job security would last as long as my software performed. But I did put my fully updated bungalow on the market and made a nice profit. So, I moved in with Mom and Dad and kept working, but worked from home and tried to bank all my pay."

"Then your grandma died unexpectedly and Ed gave you their house?"

"You got it. I can basically retire and live on my investments for a while. But, I figured I'd fix this place up and then freelance." She paused and looked over at him, "Life has been too good to me. I have a nice nest egg and now this house. Something is going to go wrong. I just know it."

Ben remarked, "Don't be like that. Sometimes you just get blessings."

Jasmine sighed, "I hope you're right, but I woke up this morning thinking this was all too good to be true. I don't know anyone else who has enough money to pay off their house before they're thirty."

The talking quieted down for a bit, but then Jasmine giggled and made a big production of meeting him in the middle of the wall. They continued working and chatting through the rest of the afternoon.

Before long they had nearly demo'd all the plaster in the smallest bedroom upstairs. Ben was working on the last few feet in the corner farthest from the door, while Jasmine had finished her last bit. He looked over and saw her standing still holding the crowbar in one hand as the other end rested on the floor, and rubbing her lower back with her other hand.

She seemed interested in watching him work. He considered telling her to come over and help him when they both heard the oven's timer go off downstairs. She remarked,

"That's dinner. Great. I'm starved. How 'bout you?"

Ben ran his arm across his forehead to swipe the sweat away, "Starved and hot. Can we eat outside, you think?"

"Sure. I think so. I spotted the old picnic table out under the pine tree by the garden when I was rifling through the garage. You can head out there with something cool to drink and I'll dish up the steaks."

Ben nodded and motioned her to lead him downstairs. They shared a delicious steak dinner with roasted veggies and green salad in the dusky night. Before the mosquitoes got too bad, they were back upstairs working.

★★★

The morning was sunny and looked like it would be hot later. Ben pulled his cooler down the back yard and sat it under the tree where it would stay cool in the shade.

"God, Jasmine. You've got to be crazy restoring this monstrosity! I can't believe you're wasting a penny of your money on this dump." Ben heard the loud voice as he came around the back of the house. He looked over to the driveway and saw a brand new Cadillac parked behind Jasmine's truck, and a slick dude in khakis and an ironed polo shirt standing next to it. As he moved closer he could see Jasmine facing the guy with her back to him. *She sure looks good today in those short shorts and that lacy top.* He thought. As usual, Jasmine looked fresh and lovely in the morning, while he was already dirty and gritty by the time she left the house.

She spotted him by the time he'd reached his truck parked to the side of hers. "Hey Ben. Come meet Ryan. He's an old work buddy who came up to see me." Ryan's perfect coif didn't move as he formally stepped forward to shake his hand. Ben was glad his hands, though rough from mixing mortar, were at least clean. Training as a gentleman at his mother's hand made him speak, "Good to meet you."

"Likewise. So, what can you do to save this place?" Ryan asked.

Ben was happy to dislike him, but tried to be polite as he ignored his deriding tone. "We're doing what we can. Thankfully, the bricks are holding up and are still strong after more than a century. We've reinforced them on the inside with parging and now I'm starting on the mortar."

"I see." Ryan then turned to Jasmine, "Well at least Victorians hold their value and you'll get a good price when you sell."

Ben watched Jasmine's face. He tried to tamp down his worry about her answer. But, she surprised him.

"Ryan, as I've told you many times before...Even if I decide to move back to Salt Lake or Provo one day, I can't see myself ever selling this place. My mother was born here, and I spent my best times here. I wonder if you can understand that."

Ryan sniffed. Ben couldn't tell whether he was miffed or just bored.

Ryan said, "Well, you know that you and I will never agree about the joys of living in the boondocks regardless of who lives there too." Abruptly he changed the subject, "So... Can I count on you for the banquet next month?"

Jasmine sighed. "No, Ryan. I sold all my formals. I don't intend to ever attend a SYMTEQ party ever again. I told you that last month when I left the Provo office. What will it take for you and Jamal to understand that I have fully curtailed my SYMTEQ activities to troubleshooting only?"

"I know. I know. We were just hoping that you'd come to this final mixer so Crosby can meet you. You know his firm has begun to spend millions on the system you helped design. He's wanted to meet you for weeks now."

Jasmine cut him off, "You mean someone showed him my picture and you want to dangle me in front of your biggest client ever like I was a bonus for him spending so much." Ben was shocked by Jasmine's angry face and tone as she finished, "For the final time, Ryan, I will not whore for you. Get the hell off my land and don't come back!"

Before he or Ryan could recover, Jasmine had slammed the screen door on the porch and was gone inside.

Ben looked to Ryan, who held up his hand. Ryan said, "Long story. I'm off."

After he pulled away, Ben knocked on the screen door, "Jasmine, can I come in?"

He heard a faint "Fine." echo from the back of the house.

He found her in the kitchen. She was standing at the sink stiff in every muscle. "Are you okay? What was that all about? I take it SYMTEQ is your old company and Ryan was your boss?"

She didn't turn to face him, but she did answer, "Yes, Ryan was one of my bosses. It takes longer to explain than I'd like, but in essence, I designed a killer software for our best client. He kept coming back and I thought things were fine, until he cornered me at our client Christmas party. Turns out, he truly liked the software, but was sure that a woman couldn't have designed it. Somewhere he'd gotten the idea that I was in fact Ryan's office bunny and that my picture was on the software packet as a way to entice male clients. He'd figured that since he'd paid a million dollars that year for the software, my personal services should be included in our contract."

"That's sick. What a creep. What did you do?"

"Well, I threw my drink on him, and set him straight, then went to Jamal, Ryan's partner and my other boss. Jamal handled it well. He cleared up the confusion and helped the customer save face, while helping him understand he was way off base. But after that, Ryan convinced him that I'd led the guy on. Things got tense and the discomfort is partly why I quit and went freelance. Ever since Jamal and Ryan have been at odds with each other. I think it's due to their embarrassment over the situation. I was their first and best female programmer. Ryan has been trying to get me to go to one last party or mixer so the guy can either apologize or try again. Then last time I saw them they said another client wanted to meet me. Apparently this other client wants to meet "the girl from the package" too. They've been pressuring me to go to their mixers ever since. I've told both Jamal and Ryan 'no' plenty of times, and I figure today was Ryan's last ditch attempt to work me over one more time trying to suck me back in." She shook her head.

Ben wasn't sure what to say, but he did his best. "Well, I'm glad you got away. It's too bad guys still think that money lets them get anything they want. Can I do anything to help?"

Jasmine turned around. "You know, you can." She stepped closer to him, "Can you give me a hug? I haven't hugged a good guy in a long time."

Ben was shocked, but glad to comply. Holding her in his arms was amazing; Jasmine fit him perfectly. She was just the right height and soft and curvy all over.

She broke contact first. "Thanks. I needed that. I'm going to make some phone calls and then go into town. Do you need anything?"

"Nope, I'm fine. Will you be back in time for lunch? Mom wanted me to ask you."

"Sure, I can make it back for lunch. Twelve as usual?"

"You got it. And, in the meantime, don't let asses like Ryan or that customer get you down. There are plenty of good guys out there."

"Yeah, like you and Miguel. Thanks for reminding me."

"Anytime. See you later today."

Ben thought of Jasmine all that day. The brickwork was progressing nicely. The inside parging coatings were complete and all the steel reinforcement bars were secured. Miguel had finished the roof, so as soon as Ben finished the mortar, the work could move inside to the HVAC, walls, and floors.

He'd been trying for weeks to decide how he could convince Jasmine to go out on a date with him. A hug seemed like a good start.

★★★

Ben rolled over and looked at his alarm clock. *Have I really been working with Jasmine on the Nelson house for ten weeks?* He was wide-awake as he watched the digital numbers switch from five fifty-nine to six o'clock and the alarm went off. He sighed and reached over to cancel the alarm. *What's another sleepless night after all? It's not like I'll ever get Jasmine to notice me as a guy she could date.* Ben examined the dark shadows under his eyes that matched the shadows on his jaw in the mirror. Carefully he shaved and then started his shower with cold water in an effort to revive himself. A half-hour later, he was clean, dressed, and ready for the day when he appeared at his mother's breakfast table. If she noticed his tired eyes, she didn't say anything as she heaped steaming pancakes and sausage on his plate.

Ben had swallowed his first bite and had started chewing his second when his mom turned back to face him across the kitchen. He chewed as he watched her warily. After a few heartbeats, she spoke,

"Are you sure you want to get involved with Jasmine?"

Ben choked, "What are you talking about, Mom? I thought you liked Jasmine."

"Well, Mrs. Netter spotted that slick dude in his Cadillac over there again last night. She called me this morning just to let me know he didn't leave until two AM."

Ben met his mother's stare. Her lips were turned down and frown lines deeply etched across her face. "Mom. Jasmine doesn't like the Ryan guy that drives the Cadillac. You know that. She told you herself."

His mother looked unconvinced, "Well, then why has his car been over there three times this week? What's going on between you and her? You know she's probably only being nice to us while you are working on the house."

"I am sure you're wrong about her, Mom."

"Regardless, please be careful. We don't know anything about Jasmine. Your dad barely remembers her mom, and you don't know whether or not she's just playing you for a fool even if she is Ed's granddaughter."

"Mom. You know no one ever goes out to be a fool for some girl purposely. Besides, Jasmine's not like that, and I am not into her that way. So can you leave off, okay?" Ben hoped his mom would let the "Jasmine" issue lie.

His mother looked unconvinced, but must have decided she'd get no further this morning, so she said, "All right, fine. But, I will ask Jasmine about the Cadillac guy and get the truth out of her once and for all." She turned back to the sink to start hot water for dishes.

Ben was grateful he didn't have to answer more questions. *I hope Mom is just being overprotective. I don't know what I'll do if she decides to dislike Jasmine.* He focused on finishing his pancakes as he planned out the day's activities on the Nelson house.

★★★

Jasmine hadn't known that Jamal would send Ryan to Utah State University in Logan, Utah to personally oversee the company's latest applicants at the at the spring career fair at the college. SYMTEQ liked to have a big booth at all the local colleges' spring job fairs and the HR staff worked hard to ensure they had the pick of the computer students for their staff.

Ryan had came to Logan last weekend and was staying there for the next ten days while the SYMTEQ staff prepared for, conducted interviews at, and headhunted Logan dry of computer personnel during the job fair. Logan was an easy hour drive to Penrose, and three days before, Ryan had showed up at Jasmine's at ten PM just after Ben had left for the night.

Ryan had come bearing gifts for Jasmine hoping to soften her up. Besides a beautiful formal gown in just her size, he had two five-hundred-dollar cards, one for Chevron gas and the other, a pre-paid Visa card to cover her expenses so she could come to their fall mixer. He'd been contrite and kind, and promised that she could keep these items and just "think it over". He then asked her permission to come see her the next night for her answer.

Jasmine had left the dress hanging above the window in the front room by her computer and left the cards nearby.

She'd stared at them and mulled over the situation with Ryan all the next day. It was Sunday, so she only saw Ben at church, and didn't have to explain a ball gown to him. That night, Ryan came as planned, and seemed to take her refusal well. He took back the cards, but told her to keep the dress as a good-will gesture from him and Jamal. Reluctantly, Jasmine took the dress upstairs and hid it in the master closet behind her other clothes. That room was fully finished and would be her bedroom once she and Ben had finished painting the rest of the upstairs and refinished the repaired hardwood floors.

Yesterday, Monday, had been a good day. She and Ben had placed the final coat of finish on the upstairs hall. This meant that once they laid the vinyl in the upstairs bath and reset the toilet, the upstairs would be finished. They'd gone into town to celebrate by having dinner at the bowling alley in Tremonton and Ben had dropped her off at nine PM. Jasmine had got into her pajamas and had powered on her laptop to work on some freelance programming work. When she heard a car pull into the drive, the clock on her computer showed one-nineteen AM. Thinking it was an emergency or something, she answered the knock on the front door. It wasn't Ben, or any of her family, but Ryan.

Ryan tried to smile at her, but his face turned into a sneer in the light from the porch's overhead light as he snarled, "So you won't come back to us, huh, you bitch. Jamal told me how you sold him all your stock. You owe us. You owe *me!*" With that he rushed into the house, pushing her back into the room.

Jasmine backed away further and tried to think of how she could escape from him, mentally measuring whether the pantry door was sturdy enough to hold him away from her. She glanced to her computer where her cell phone sat. Ryan saw her eyes move and noticed the phone too.

"No way, bitch."

Before she could react, Ryan backhanded her, knocking her to the floor where she landed hard on her tailbone and bouncing her head against the floor. He stood between her raised knees where he crouched and leaned down to look her in the eye, "I'll show you just who's boss of you."

Jasmine's jaw throbbed where Ryan's hand had caught her, and the back of her head ached where it had hit the floor. She was too dazed to stop Ryan in any meaningful way when he knelt down fully and grabbed her by the throat. Desperately she clawed at his wrists and arms as he began choking her. Soon black spots appeared in her eyes, and then a curtain of darkness came at the edges of her vision and eventually filled her sight. She didn't know it, but Ryan had continued choking her for a few seconds after she passed out.

Jasmine came to sometime later disoriented, sore, and hoping she was still alive. She found she was laying on her back in the front room. The light was off, and the front door was standing open. A cool night breeze was blowing past her, and she wondered whether it had woke her up. Gingerly she rolled to her side, where she rested for a few seconds as the waves of pain from her head and neck washed over her. She made it to all fours, but felt too dizzy to stand, so she crawled the ten feet to the hall bath under the stairs. She managed to open the door from her knees and inched forward to the sink. Ben had secured the sink that floated from the wall with thick carriage bolts and told her a six-hundred-pound gorilla couldn't pull it down. Jasmine prayed he was right, as she grasped the sink and used it as leverage to pull herself upright.

Jasmine held on to the sink as she hung her head down waiting for the dizziness to pass and her knees to stop shaking. She eventually turned on the light and examined herself in the mirror. She had a nasty red mark that would be a bruise on the side of her jaw from Ryan's hit, and clear choke marks from his fingers around her neck like a macabre necklace. She began to shake all over and couldn't stop the tears that began running down her cheeks.

She walked unsteadily into the kitchen using her hands against the hall walls to keep steady. She got a bag of frozen peas to hold on her head while she debated calling for help on the kitchen phone. The stove clock showed the time as three thirty-four AM. She'd been out for nearly two hours. She leaned against the wall next to the 1970's banana phone mounted on the wall at eye level. She held the peas against the back of her head as she used her free hand to pick up the receiver. At the dial tone, she hesitated. *Call 9-1-1 or Ben?* She went to speak and no sound came out. She tried again, but still couldn't speak; only croaks and wheezes came out her throat and it hurt to talk. Her throat felt burned like she'd thrown up for hours. Wheezing, she hung up the phone. *I give up. No calling tonight.*

She grabbed a bag of frozen corn, the only other frozen bag in her freezer, and made her way carefully to her laptop and cell phone in the front room. Feeling dizzy, she held the corn and peas in one hand while she grasped the cellphone in the other.

She turned and made it to the cot. As she lay carefully on her side, Jasmine arranged the corn behind her head and nestled the peas against her throat as she punched in her pass-code to text Ben. *Ben can come over here and call the cops for me. Please be up, Ben. Please hear your phone.* Jasmine's fingers matched the shaky feeling in her stomach as she typed in "Help. I need you. Please come here." on her conversation stream to Ben. She hit send and waited. Minutes passed, and no response from Ben. *Should I text Mom and Dad? NO. They'll panic and it's a three-hour drive up here. I'll wait for Ben. If he doesn't come soon, I'll call him and the cops in the morning.*

She was able to sleep for a couple of hours. The sunlight from the eastern window woke her up. Jasmine looked around the room. Pain and fear overwhelmed her. She knew Ryan would panic and take off, probably to Mexico or something. *He has to know I'd call the cops and he'd be busted.* If he didn't run, he'd probably come back to work her over again today or tomorrow. Jasmine worried, she didn't know what Ryan could do, but it would be bad. She knew he had a terrible temper, and he wasn't likely to let her nail him for assault. She had a little time to be ready for him. Feeling worn out, Jasmine closed her eyes and cried silently for a few minutes.

She recovered and looked at the clock. It showed five-thirty AM. *Ben's not here yet, and hasn't responded to my text, so it's clear he hadn't got it last night.* Jasmine weighed her options, and decided to stay in bed. *Ben will be here momentarily.* He aimed to start work by eight AM each day, but sometimes got there as early as six AM depending on his mood or the day's plans. Too sore to get up and close the front door or make her way back to the kitchen, Jasmine laid back in her cot, slid the thawed vegetable bags onto the floor and hoped to sleep until Ben arrived for their morning's work.

Later, the sun woke her up again. It was much brighter now. She lay on the cot staring at the ceiling now fully lit by the sun as she tried to not cry again. Her throat ached both inside from her tears and outside from Ryan's rough handling.

Why didn't I just shoot him the first time he came back here last week? I know Ben would have let me borrow his pistol.

Jasmine was trying to decide to get up and call the cops when she heard Ben's truck pull in the drive. *At least I hope that's Ben. If not, I don't care. I can't fight Ryan off again feeling like this.*

★★★

Ben slammed his truck door shut, still feeling ticked off over his Mom's lecture. He took one step towards the house and stopped. *Damn. Forgot my phone. I hope I left it in the truck last night. It wasn't in the house when I left this morning.* He reopened his door and grabbed his cell phone from his charging spot below the dash. He saw no missed calls, but a text. He'd check it in a minute. He needed to see Jasmine. His mom's lecture was riding him hard. He needed to speak to Jasmine and clear his mind of his mom's suspicions before he did anything else this morning. He pocketed the phone and walked to the front door.

The open door caught Ben's attention. *Her front door's open?* He thought as worry lines wrinkled on his forehead. Jasmine would leave the back or side doors open to let in the breeze now and then, but she hated leaving the front door open. She didn't want folks to see her bedroom just off the foyer until she'd made the bed. Plus, it faced the highway and the noisy morning commuter traffic would wake her up. That it was open this early was not like her. Ben peeked around the side of the house to see if the truck was in its usual spot. It was. He carefully pushed in the door. No lights were on, but the sun was shining in through the transept window above the door. He edged in the room, ready to back out if Jasmine was sleeping or not dressed. What he saw had him across the room and kneeling by her cot in two seconds.

"God, Jasmine! Are you okay?" Ben gently touched her shoulder to see if she was awake as he spoke. His eyes took in the horrible bruises on her throat, the redness in her eyes, and the nasty bruise on her jaw. Someone had beat her up and apparently tried to choke her. Jasmine opened her eyes, she tried to speak, and Ben caught:

"You came. You're here. Thank Heavens." Jasmine made to sit up and get her phone, but stopped and closed her eyes and moved her hand to the back of her head. She looked to be in pain.

Ben spoke, "Don't talk, honey. I can see you're hurt. You need medical attention. Did you call the cops?"

Jasmine started crying again. She held up her cell phone. "Can't talk. Texted you last night. Waiting for…"

"Oh my God. You're my text! I left my phone in the truck." Ben went to stand up as he heard Jasmine say,

"Hurts…"

"I'll get you some ice."

Ben stood up and saw the thawed bags of frozen peas and corn by his feet. He scooped them up and threw them in the sink as he opened Jasmine's freezer. It didn't have an icemaker and Jasmine hated homemade ice, so the trays were gone. It looked like the corn and peas were the only frozen veggies she had, all that was left in the freezer was a handful of Otter-Pops frozen ice snacks. Ben grabbed one. He figured it would help soothe Jasmine's throat as he went to the bathroom to soak some towels in cold water.

He returned to the front room. Handing Jasmine the Otter-Pop, he said, "Here, suck on this, it will help your throat. These towels will help your head and neck until I can get some icepacks. I'll make some calls."

Jasmine took the ice snack willingly and held one of the towels against her throat with her other hand. Ben pulled her computer chair over to the cot and sat in it as he examined her head to figure out why it hurt. He found the goose egg on the back of Jasmine's head and held the other towel to it as he called his mom and then nine-one-one.

His mom arrived with icepacks five minutes before the EMTs from the Thatcher-Penrose Volunteer Fire Department arrived. Ten minutes later the Box Elder county sheriff and a deputy arrived to begin the investigation.

Ben stood in the hallway to the kitchen watching Jasmine and his mom talk. In the past two hours, he'd watched the EMTs do what they could for Jasmine and help the sheriff deputy document her injuries in photographs. The deputy had called in a victim's counselor to advise Jasmine of her rights as he left to call in Ryan's information from his patrol truck's radio. The sheriff took Jasmine's official statement and went through the house and outside it looking for evidence.

The cops found the formal Ryan had given Jasmine shredded upstairs in the master bedroom. One of her kitchen knives was up there too, and it appeared that Ryan had used it to shred the dress. The Box Elder CSI staff was coming to bag everything up and further document Jasmine and the state of the house. The deputy also canvassed the neighbors and took their statements about when the Cadillac had been at

Jasmine's house and for how long. *Too bad that gravel driveways don't keep tire tracks.* Ben thought.

Jasmine looked tired. He was tired. *I need to get out of here and get Jasmine out of here too.* He wanted to choke Ryan until his throat matched hers. Over his mom's head, he saw the CSI van pull in the drive, and he moved into the room. "Okay, Mom, the CSI guys are here. Why don't you head home, and I'll bring Jasmine down shortly?"

"Okay, son. You'll check in when you get home?"

"Sure will."

Ben's mom then addressed Jasmine, "Rest and feel better, honey. Let us take care of you until they catch that guy."

Jasmine nodded, and Ben's mom left the house.

As she left, the sheriff deputy came back in followed by two CSI officers in uniform wearing gloves. Ben helped Jasmine sit up while they took more pictures of her. They were very interested to see whether she showed defensive wounds on her hands and arms. They found some bruises on her wrists and the outside of her lower arms. They then switched cameras and took some infrared photographs to show any bruising not yet visible. Finally they picked at and swabbed her fingernails for Ryan's tissue. They hoped that her scratches were not only visible on Ryan, but that she had his DNA under her fingernails.

When everyone cleared her to go, Ben moved in and swooped Jasmine with her blanket up in to his arms. "If anyone needs her, she'll be at my place. You have my number. Please lock the door when you're done."

With that Ben carried Jasmine out of the house into the bright afternoon sunlight. "You okay going to my place, or do you want to stay at Mom's until your family comes to get you?"

He barely heard her quiet croak, "Yours, please." as he gently sat her on the passenger seat of the truck.

At home, Ben asked, "Do you want to rest on the couch down here, or upstairs on the bed?"

Jasmine's eyes were tightly shut with pain, but she managed, "Bed."

Ryan carried her smoothly up the stairs and considered his two bedrooms. One was stuffed with the business's papers, files, and computers, and other had his bed, the *only* bed in the house. Grateful that he'd made it this morning and had cleaned up after himself, Ben lay Jasmine down gently on the bed on top the covers. She rolled slightly to rest on her side, and he nestled his best pillow under her neck. He then pulled his grandma's quilt from its resting spot on his blanket chest and spread it over Jasmine. He stood up and watched her settle. Soon, she'd nestled down into the blanket and quilt and began breathing deeply. Ben pocketed her cell phone and went downstairs to consult with his mom. They needed to plan.

***

Jasmine awoke in a warm and comfy bed, and realized she didn't know where she was. Disoriented, she sat up and realized her head spun slightly. She waited, and soon her world righted. She breathed in deeply and felt her head clear. She had a residual headache, but it was much milder than the one that accompanied her to sleep. Her normally fast-processing brain was back. She could remember exactly what happened over the past thirty-six hours, and knew she was in Ben's house and in his bed. *I know there's nothing much I have to do right now…that is, until Mom and Dad get here, but I wonder… should I get up and go downstairs?* Jasmine felt a wave of anxiety wash over her. She wasn't sure how to face Ben.

Last night, as she lay in bed praying that Ryan would not come back, and that Ben would come over, she'd realized that while she'd accept comfort from either of her parents, she desperately wanted *Ben's* comfort, no one else's. In fact as she sat here, in his bed, Jasmine realized she didn't want to leave it. *I don't want to leave this room or this house, and it's not for fear of going back to my house. I want to stay with Ben.* Jasmine couldn't even think it, but part of her added "forever" to her thought.

Vignettes of times she'd spent with Ben played in her mind. Many meals, innumerable jokes, and hours of hard-working companionship swamped her. She could picture Ben in all sorts of poses and postures and hear his voice saying anything. She could feel the roughened texture of his hands and the soft silkiness of the hair at the base of his neck in her fingertips. She'd found herself staring at his shoulders lately and she loved watching the play of the muscles across his back as he lifted a heavy object. But, until last night, she hadn't realized the friendly feelings she'd had for him had turned into something else.

All of a sudden, Jasmine heard the doorbell sound and voices downstairs. *OMG, that's probably Mom and Dad. How am I going to face them? How do I tell them that my feelings for Ben have overridden any concerns I had about Ryan?* Resolved to do her best to do and say what felt right, Jasmine stood up, folded her blanket and Ben's quilt, laid them on the bed, and moved to the door. She followed the hall to the top of the stairs, keeping one hand against the wall for support. As she grasped the handrail, Ben came into view coming up the steps. The bedroom light shown down the hall and illuminated his face against the darkened stairwell behind him.

His eyes were full of concern and worry as he met her look. "Are you okay? Should you be up? Do you need me to carry you downstairs?" His voice followed its usual brisk cadence, but she could hear a shakiness in it that betrayed his worry for her.

Staring down at him, Jasmine felt love wash through her. As her mouth opened to answer his questions as he reached the last riser, without conscious intent she heard herself say, "I am just fine. I feel much better, but before we go downstairs…" Jasmine paused, not sure how to express the feelings that overwhelmed her.

"Well, what?" Ben closed the gap between them and stood staring down at her, close enough that she could feel his body heat.

Jasmine took tiny steps to close the scant inches between them and placed her hands palm down on his chest as she tilted her face up to his. "Well, before we go downstairs to plan out what we're going to do about Ryan or my house, I wanted to tell you that I learned something important last night when I realized that you were the first person I wanted to call..." Jasmine's courage faltered for a second, and she saw Ben's mouth open to say something. Her fingers covered his mouth, "No. I need to say this, if I can get the words right... Um. I realized that I didn't want Mom or Dad, or even the cops. I wanted *you* there. I wanted *you* with me to take care of me, protect me, and to take out Ryan if needs be. I wanted *you*. I realized that I... I love you." Jasmine felt nervousness blush across her face. She'd never told anybody that she loved them before.

★★★

Did she just say that? OMG. Am I really upstairs in my house looking at the woman I adore, and did she just say she loves me? Ben stared at Jasmine as her fingers dropped from his lower jaw. Even in the dim light, he could see she was blushing and embarrassed. She looked down. He wasn't sure what to say. His heart was thumping so hard; he wondered whether she could feel it across the inch or so between them. He heard Jasmine's dad's voice from behind him,

"Ben, is Jasmine okay? Are you guys coming downstairs?"

Before he could answer, Jasmine spoke, hoarsely but a clearly, "Hey, Daddy. We'll be down in a minute. I'm moving slow."

"Okay, honey. Your mother and I are just chatting with Ben's parents. Take your time."

Ben kept staring at Jasmine as the words finally formed in his brain so he could speak them, "So. You love me, huh?"

Jasmine's eyebrows wrinkled like they did whenever she wasn't sure about something, "Yes. I think so. That's what I said." Her other hand dropped from his chest and she lifted her foot preparing to step back away from him.

"Not so fast, missy." Ben spoke as he moved his arms around her and pulled her close, halting any retreat. "You don't know how many times I've prayed and hoped to hear you say those words. Jasmine, baby, I love you too." Before she could answer him, he swooped down his head and caught her lips in a kiss.

They were still kissing when Ben's mother appeared at the top of the stairs. Her voice broke them out of their embrace as she hollered back down the stairs, "No, guys, they're fine. They're just making out at the top of the stairs. Looks like we have a bit more than assault and attempted murder to talk about."

8

Max & Leslie

Max was in a bind. He had five kids and a newspaper to take care of. He didn't know how he was going to do it. In the six months since his beloved wife Joanna had died after fifteen years of marriage, he'd exhausted the skills of all the local teenage babysitters, alienated his mother and mother-in-law, and worked his sister Lucy to death taking care of his fourteen-year-old, six-year old, and eight-month-old daughters and twelve-year-old twin sons. His oldest definitely was having a hard time taking care of her baby sister and keeping up with her schoolwork. Angie was just too young, and Max couldn't dump all that responsibility on the kid for long. He needed real help. His kids needed adult supervision. His paper needed its editor. And, the house needed a total cleaning overhaul. Max needed a miracle or a basket of them. He started praying hard and hoping God would take mercy on him, for once.

★★★

Leslie was down on her luck. Moving to a new town without a job and only the possessions her car would hold just may get the best of her. She hoped and prayed things would work out. Portland was beautiful. It was so green and vibrant after Phoenix. Both Oregon and Arizona were miles away from her hometown in rural Arkansas though. When her mom had told her dad off and moved her to Phoenix when she was ten, Leslie had been sure that move would kill her. Twenty-five years and a dozen moves later, Leslie knew better. She would survive this.

Leslie had finished high school in Phoenix, went to UNLV on an academic scholarship, and had graduated with honors after the typical four years. She'd worked her tail off in Vegas at a bar and at the college bookstore to pay for room and board. She'd earned a degree in early childhood education and had hoped to go on to get a doctorate degree. Then she'd met Barry, married, and had settled back in Phoenix to live the perfect life. That plan lasted six years. In that time, she ran a daycare out of their house to supplement Barry's income as a paralegal to help him finish law school. The same month that he'd passed the Arizona bar exam, they'd found out that Leslie's endometriosis had destroyed any chances that they'd ever have a baby of their own. Leslie was devastated and figured that Barry was too, until one day he came home in a new, red convertible and announced they were through.

She'd cleaned up respectably in the divorce. Leslie hadn't helped her lawyer ex through law school without picking up some stuff. She'd got the house and the red convertible, and Barry paid them off in exchange for a no-alimony agreement. He also agreed when Leslie brokered for a cash settlement. With the cash, she figured she could grow her daycare business to the point where she could purchase a separate building, hire a staff, and then get her P. H., D. She made it through the plan until she had the new building, five successfully years of business with her staff of eight, and her master's degree, then the economy crashed. Leslie lost the business, liquidated the building and ended up selling the house to pay the rest of the debt.

She traded the now "classic" convertible for a dependable sedan and used most of her remaining cash to say goodbye to Phoenix. Her best friend from college lived in Portland and offered Leslie a couch and a garage for the summer to allow Leslie some time to find a life for herself. Katy had promised that she could even do piercings for the hippies who frequented her husband's tattoo parlor for money if all else failed.

★★★

Max hung up the phone and felt a glimmer of hope for the first time in a long time. *Lucy has forgiven me. That's something positive today.* Worry had overtaken his life from the morning when he'd held his fifth child in his arms and learned that his wife would be staying the hospital. The doctors had found the cancer during the pregnancy and the birth had caused Joanna to hemorrhage when the cancerous tumor ruptured. They thought the uterine tumor must have formed during the pregnancy and grew quickly. The doctors tried chemo, but avoided radiation hoping the chemo would be enough, but Joanna still died. The cancer ate away at her at the same pace her baby daughter grew. His sister Lucy was single so she moved in and stayed through Joanna's passing to help them with the house and kids.

Lucy was the one who'd suggested Max hire a housekeeper and a nanny, and joked he ought to get married instead. Max normally appreciated Lucy's dark humor, a trait that they had both inherited from their dad, but not that day. Joanna's absence was an ulcer on his heart and hurt like a canker sore soaked in pineapple juice. He squelched thoughts of the last promise he'd made to Joanna before she'd died. He'd promised her he'd not shut down his heart, and that he would marry again. *Joanna would have me married again before she was in the ground. And now Lucy's started harassing me to get married.* That day Max yelled at Lucy. He'd shocked his kids and ensured that when Lucy left for the day, she left for good. Only later did he realize that his anger at his sister stemmed from guilt over not wanting to fulfill his promise to Joanna.

Max used his contacts at the paper to search for help and found an amazing housekeeper in Danny. Danny was built like a defensive lineman, but moved like a ballerina and loved cleaning houses. He'd joked during the job interview that he'd make a great houseboy. Max wondered if Danny was making a pass at him, and stared at him not sure what he meant. Then Danny explained how he'd grown up helping his mom clean houses for a living. He then explained that he was dating a girl who worked as a physical trainer for a cruise line. Since she was gone for weeks at a time, and Danny hated living in their apartment by himself, he was looking for a job as live-in help. Danny's only request of Max was that he be allowed periodic long weekends to enjoy time with his girl when she was in town.

After Danny had worked for him awhile, Max had taken up Lucy's suggestion to get a nanny. Danny had all he could do, and the kids still needed more support. He suggested Max contact a local care broker who could hook Max up with someone for temporary babysitting or a full-time nanny. He had a running joke, where he'd tell Max to put an ad in the local college newspaper for a nanny and see who showed up. After a few weeks of trying out four different nannies who became overwhelmed by Max's five kids, the service had yet to find someone capable of taking care of his brood.

★★★

Leslie thought she'd hate tattoos. She knew she hated nose-rings ever since her seventeen-year-old niece had put a tiny bullring through her nose. But, she found out she was a great tattoo artist. She had a steady hand with the needles, and running a daycare had somehow taught her how to draw amazing things. She'd had little luck finding other employment so far, so she took Katy's offer to help in her husband's tattoo parlor.

She worked three days a week plus Saturdays for Katy's husband and had pierced and gauged enough body parts to know that piercing wasn't for her in the long-term. Leslie finished prepping the area and squeezed the trigger, which finished her latest piercing. As she took payment and watched the guy walk carefully out of the shop, she thought, *It's ironic that Katy was one of only two of my friends who knew that I worked doing piercings in the mall back then. Only Katy would think that a job I worked at sixteen to finance my trips to my old boyfriend's concerts could be turned into a career for the thirty-five-year-old failed daycare owner. Oh well, at least I enjoy the tattoos.*

Katy felt Leslie's pain and frustration over her lack of daycare options and kept researching the child–care market around her Portland neighborhood. She'd found a caregiver service that brokered deals for people needing care and care providers. Katy and Leslie agreed this company would be a good fit, because they worked with all levels of care, from a couple hours babysitting jobs to full-time, permanent, live-in nanny duties. Leslie hoped she could work both as a nanny part-time and as a tattoo artist for a time until she could find a place and open her own daycare. She'd use the time to build up her savings and decide whether she needed a career change, and if so what she'd do.

★★★

Danny approached Max's incredibly clean office at the newspaper. Max suited his Portland environment, and had gone paperless in his process with the sole exception of the actual news–printed pages. The desk was clean as usual, but Max seemed to be having a bad day. His head lay facedown on the desk and he appeared to be flexing his shoulders as he sat in the chair. Danny had seen this stance amongst the chaos that was Max's home kitchen, so he recognized the signs of one of Max's "I've had enough!" moments. Tentatively, he asked, "Uh. Max, are you okay? Can I ask you about a listing I found?"

Max answered without lifting his head from his arms, so he sounded a bit muffled, "I'm fine. But I don't want to hear about some sweet young thing down on her luck…I need a competent general who can keep a teenage nightmare in line at the same time she nurtures my poor infant daughter. Did you find anyone like that, Danny? Also, I hope my mother is with my progeny, since you are here."

Danny was quick to assure Max about his kids before answering his other question. "Yes, your mom is there. They were making pizza when I left." He moved closer and held out a slip of paper. "Well, I'm not sure, but this may be the right "body" for you. See I found a listing today at the care center that looks the same as one I saw in the student services building at the college. And, it's your standard, "Ex-daycare owner ready to take on a nanny position" type ad, but I recognize the phone number. It's the number to Cracked-Up Tattoos."

"Are you telling me you found me an ex-daycare person who also does tattoos?" Max still didn't raise his head, but his tone turned sarcastic, "Great. I can save money and let him tattoo my kids for free."

"Well, that's why I wanted to talk to you about it in person. See, Cracker, the owner of the tattoo shop, is an old buddy of Dad's. He and Dad were in the military together. After they both retired, Cracker moved up here from Vegas with his old lady and they've been doing tats ever since. But Katy, that's Mrs. Cracker, is also a lunch lady. She was looking for a job that had heath insurance. Cracker has the VA, but she has nil, so she started working for the school. Since she needed a flexible schedule, she…"

Max cut him off and looked up at him, "So she became a lunch lady. You think a lunch lady who knows her way around a tattoo parlor can handle my kids?"

"Well that's just it. The ad sounds like Katy wrote it, and maybe she wrote it for one of her lunch-lady friends, but it says, "Ask for Leslie." I admit I was intrigued by the idea of a tattoo guy named Leslie running your kids around. I mean, the jokes write themselves, but I think this may be the solution. I know Cracker and Katy and they're good, dependable folks despite the wildness in their lifestyle. And, this ad was in two places, which tells me this Leslie is probably serious."

Max muttered, "Or desperate." Danny saw a bit of hope in his eyes as Max continued, "Well, going the traditional route hasn't worked, and the readers of this newspaper are more into food than babies, making my own ads useless, so I'll trust your thoughts this time." Max stood up and held out his hand, "Give me the ad. I'll go over and talk to Leslie, and meet you at home."

Danny felt a little concern, "But, Max you aren't dressed for that area...I mean, Cracked-Up is clean, but you hardly look like a guy needing a tattoo. Now if it was tonight and you were dead drunk, you'd be perfect in your slacks."

Max waved him off, "It's time I took an interest in fixing my life instead of letting you, my mom, my mom-in-law, or my sister do it. This will give me a chance to see what you have all experienced. Besides, one of my regular freelancers asked me about doing a story on Cracked-Up tats, so I can use the recon."

★★★

Max texted his secretary, who was manning the newspaper's phones from home today since it was Saturday, telling her that he'd be out of the office for a few hours, and drove over to Cracked-Up Tattoos. The tattoo parlor was in a small row of shops along a tree-lined thoroughfare just outside of Portland's city limits in a hip neighborhood. It sat between an herbalist's shop and a vintage clothing/used clothing dealer. It wasn't a bad neighborhood, but with his short hair, clean shave, and dress shirt and slacks, Max looked more like a government inspector or a cop than a customer.

The newspaperman in him decided from the well-designed and executed hand-painted sign on the front window and the bright red geraniums growing in the south-facing flower box that this place boasted someone with a good visual eye. If the sign was an indication of the designer's skill, this would also be an excellent place to get a tattoo.

The door was open, and Max stepped in and saw four tattoo stations behind a small counter. All but one of the stations were empty, but he could hear music coming from a rear entrance behind the last station. He took two steps to the counter and a teenaged girl came out from the rear entrance. She quickly crossed to the counter and asked, "You here for a tattoo, mister?"

"Not today, but maybe later. I'm here to talk to Cracker about an ad he placed for Leslie."

"My dad's in the back. I'll get him." With that, the teenager turned away and returned the way she'd come.

Max relaxed his stance and wondered whether Cracker or Leslie was the teenager's dad. He passed the time waiting by watching the fourth station's activities. Although the active station was across the shop from where he stood, it was a small shop so Max had a clear view of everything except the actual tattoo which was hidden between the artist's left arm holding the skin taut, while her right hand held the needle apparatus.

Max was not surprised that it was a large guy getting a tattoo on his back, nor that it was a slender female giving the tattoo. He'd lived in Portland all his life and because of his life-long work at his family's newspaper, he was well acquainted with what was normal in Portland. This shop, it's location, the teenager, the guy getting the tattoo, and that the tattoo artist was female, were all normal to him.

The female herself was not normal for the shop. Unlike the guy and the teenager, she wasn't wearing any black. From what he could see, she was wearing a pale pink T-shirt and faded jeans. She had on a black apron like hairdressers wear to keep her clean, and was wearing rubber gloves. He could see boxes of black rubber gloves at each station, including hers, but she was using purple ones. She also was missing parts of the "traditional" tattoo artist's costume, as he understood it. She had no piercings other than the normal two that most women have in their ears. Her hair was brown, a regular brown, crayon color brown, and had no otherworldly streaks or patches. It was pulled back simply in a long braid. She wore no jewelry but did wear glasses, and she wore little or no makeup. Max could see her glasses; they were rimless with clear plastic frames, so they would distract from her looks as little as possible. *Most of the tattoo artists I've met where chunky glasses that stand out.*

As he looked closer he realized she wasn't a girl either; she was a grown woman. He couldn't tell how grown though. She sat in profile from where he stood, and though he couldn't make out the words, he could hear her quietly speaking to the guy as she worked. He saw the guy nod and the lady tattoo artist smile as they talked and decided she had a gentle manner that seemed to go well with her vocation.

Just then, a six-foot plus tall guy with a bald head, luxuriously long beard and mustache, and upright carriage came out of the back followed by the teenager. He reached Max, but turned back to tell the teenager, "Stay here at the counter so you can collect Bill's payment. Leslie's nearly done." He then reached out to shake Max's hand as he addressed him, "I'm Cracker. My daughter said you wanted to talk to me about Leslie's ad? Let's go out front and talk. I don't want to distract Leslie while she's in the middle of a tattoo." The man then led him outside. Once they stood in front of the shop window, he continued, "My wife Katy's friend Leslie came up here to make a new start, and Katy's the one who placed the ad. Do you need a nanny?"

"Yeah. A friend of mine saw the ad on campus and recognized your number, so I thought I'd come down and talk to you in person."

"Oh yeah. What friend?"

"Danny McAllister; he's my housekeeper."

Cracker nodded his head, "That's my buddy Mac's son. You're the one running him ragged with that huge house and all those kids, then."

The two men got to talking and really hit it off. Max got the best parts of Cracker's life story out of him; learning things like his marine buddies called him Cracker, because he would crack his knuckles loudly before a fight. In time, he told him about his position at the paper. Cracker knew about the paper and was thrilled to be featured in an upcoming article. Max also learned a bit about Leslie, and shared his childcare needs with Cracker. Both men agreed that the job could be a good fit for Leslie and at least would keep her employed while she worked towards her final goal of opening a daycare. They had been talking for a good half-hour when the teenager popped her head out to say, "Hey, Dad, Leslie's done and Bill wants to show off his new tat."

Cracker motioned to Max, "You should come in and see this. Bill's working on a grouping on his back, and asked Leslie to fill in a bit in the middle." They reached the station where a bare-chested and burly Bill was holding a large hand mirror up as he stood with his back facing a large mirror on the wall. "Hey, Cracker, Les did an amazing job. Mt. Hood is perfect and she captured Dad's looks perfectly." Cracker and Max made suitably appreciative remarks as they admired the tattoo. Max's eyes strayed over to Leslie. She had bundled the used needles and ink cups into a metal bowl and was cleaning the station with disinfectant. She piqued his curiosity. Cracker had told him that she was thirty-five and divorced, but had no kids, and no family up here. She looked younger than thirty-five, and moved in a graceful and capable manner. He admired her artistic talent. She had made a great tattoo on Bill's back. Plus, he was also betting on the fact that she worked in a tattoo parlor meant that she could be open-minded with his kids while being tough with their shenanigans. Then she spoke, and he learned that she had a no-nonsense and very sexy voice.

Leslie finished cleaning up and peeled off her stained gloves, "Hey Bill, let me clean up and get sterile again and I'll bandage that for the ride home." She stood up and nodded to all three men as she moved past them and went in the back. Max noticed that Leslie was tall, at least five-foot/ten-inches. After a few minutes she returned with fresh surgical gloves on her hands, a sterile bandage, and medical tape. Carefully she applied the bandage to Bill's back. When done she asked, "Bill, can you move with it like that? Will you be able to control your bike?"

"Sure thing, Miss Leslie. It feels fine, and besides, I can run my bike wrapped up like a mummy and with one finger if I had to." They all laughed at Bill's joke.

The teenager took the now-dressed Bill up front to settle up, and Cracker gestured to Leslie, who was peeling off her latest pair of gloves, "Les, this is Max Baer, the owner and editor of *Baer in the Woods*. He came by to interview me today about Cracked-Up, but he also has a personal interest in your daycare ad. Can you spare some time for him right now?"

Leslie looked up and met Max's eyes directly for the first time as she answered Cracker and peeled off her surgical gloves, "Sure can, Cracker. Katy and I aren't taking the girls out shopping until tonight." She turned to Max and held out her hand to shake his as she said, "I am free the rest of the afternoon, Mr. Baer."

Cracker went into the back after that, and his daughter plopped down on a stool behind the counter as she pulled out a phone to play with while she watched for customers. Max and Leslie sat down in her station. Max perched on the bench Bill had recently vacated and Leslie sat on her padded stool, and then Max began interviewing Leslie for his nanny job.

★★★

Leslie got out of the shower and looked in the mirror trying to decide whether or not to wear makeup over to

Max's house tonight to meet the kids. As she reached up a hand, she saw it was shaking. *No makeup tonight, missy. Your hands are shaking too badly.* For the first time in a while, Leslie stared at her reflection in the mirror trying to decide whether she was beautiful or not. Ever since her ex had decided that a woman who couldn't have babies had no worth, Leslie had been unsure of her own attractiveness. She'd dated off and on, but had never gotten close to another man since. *And then today, I meet a most handsome widower that has five children who really need a mother, and he wants me to be their nanny.* Leslie sighed.

Katy told her she was pretty and so had her mother. Her mother couldn't resist a joke though, "You look great for a thirty-five-year-old divorcee and failed business owner." Katy was her measuring stick. She was honest to a fault and had never lied to Leslie in the past, and Leslie was hoping she wasn't now when she'd said, "My God, Leslie. We're the same age, but you have no wrinkles, no gray hair, and your boobs haven't even thought about falling. You could pass for twenty-five if you tried." *Oh well. The guys at the shop look at me like I'm attractive, and Max saw me today at my barest—Wearing jeans and a T-shirt with no makeup or earrings and my hair in a braid. That's the real me anyway. I might as well be myself. Besides, it's not like Mr. Handsome would go looking to a middle-aged nanny for company.*

Leslie perked herself up by repeating her daily mantra, "You were a successful businesswoman. Your business failed because the economy turned south and your clients left the area. You can do it again. Remember, that unlike others, you were able to clear your debts so you are ready to try again as soon as you have the capital." She added a bit just for today, "And, if the kids like you, you will have a steady job that comes with room and board so you can save like crazy for that capital. Be strong, girl."

Leslie ended up dressing in a soft, fleecy sweater and newer jeans, but she added some of her favorite jewelry she'd got from a Navajo friend, liquid strings of silver that hung from her ears and throat that moved with her and shimmered in the light. She left her long hair down and omitted any makeup.

★★★

A few nights later, Danny met his girl Natalie for their monthly date. He had a lot of news and business to discuss with her. They had gotten home from dinner early and were lying snuggled up in their king-sized bed at the flat they now only shared when Natalie was on hiatus from a cruise. "Natty, I've been thinking."

"Of what, Dan?"

"Well, of switching up our living conditions."

"What do you mean?"

"Well, Max found a nanny, and she's working out great. He needed my room in the house for her, and he's moved me out to the apartment over the garage. It's bigger and better, and has a separate bedroom, a kitchen, and a full bath. And, well, I was wondering if you wanted to move in there instead of here." Danny paused. He'd moved into Natalie's place, but now here he was asking her to give it up and come move into his.

Natalie looked thoughtful, "What's the rent there?"

"Well, Max is giving me a great deal. It's just five hundred dollars a month. So I figure we could really save money, plus you don't have to worry about this place being empty while you are gone."

"Okay, baby. Let's go for it. You can take me over to see the new place tomorrow, and if I think I can live there, we'll start packing."

★★★

Leslie held baby Jane (Janie) close as she hummed to her while she vacuumed. In the past two months, she'd learned quickly to include Janie in her all her activities each day. Leslie suspected the ten-month-old was very conscious of what was happening around her and had somehow absorbed her mother's death so soon after her birth. She believed Janie felt insecure and made it a point to keep her with her at all times. Fourteen-year-old Angie, the twelve-year-old twins Fritz and William and little six-year-old Bess had all also shown signs of being motherless children when she'd moved in.

Now they all had fallen into a successful routine, and the kids were feeling secure. Danny and his girl now lived above the garage, and he worked Monday-Friday days doing the housework. Leslie had full time nanny/surrogate mommy duties twenty-four/seven and covered for Danny on the weekends. Max worked hard to give her some regular time off, alternating one all-day and one all-night evening off each week. Max had also changed up his schedule as best he could, and now teleworked on Saturdays and Sundays from the dining room to further lighten her load. Then, after he'd go to the paper on Saturday nights, Leslie would bundle the whole family and follow him. This allowed the whole family to enjoy the family business while he finished the Sunday morning special.

Max's family had run a newspaper in Portland while it was still a big lumber and shipping hub. They'd emigrated from Germany in the 1860s and had built a sprawling house that later became a compound when money was abundant. They also built a new building to hold the presses that was still in use today. Even though the paper had evolved into a locals-only special, it was still successful. Leslie had lived in Portland long enough to appreciate how Max kept the *Baer in the Woods* successful in a town that had as many tree-huggers as foodies, homeless, and millionaires. The electronic version of the paper required a minimal monthly subscription, but the paper copy was free. The electronic version went a little further on the stories, but only the paper version had coupons. Max's sponsors were more than happy to give away free copies at their stores, stands, and food trucks. Folks looking for his paper usually bought something. Folks visiting their favorite establishments often picked up a paper for a quick read and would find a valuable coupon inside. Max also kept a great advertising staff on hand so that his ad revenue remained strong.

Leslie had quickly learned that Max really needed a mom for his kids, because of the demands of the paper. His family legacy of a house and newspaper gave him prosperity, but required a lifetime to maintain. So she worked hard to keep baby Janie happy and growing while she helped the older kids with their homework and life choices so they could spend what time they could with their old man.

Leslie couldn't be happier living as she did. She fit right in the Baer household. Plus, she really enjoyed doing the light housework on Danny's nights off. It gave her a chance to pretend this house and these kids were her own. And, it helped keep her distance from Max by keeping busy.

Max and Danny seemed conscious of her needs too. They were there for her when she needed a break or had to do an errand. She could go to church on Sundays, visit with Katy and her family now and then, and even spend a weekend out if she liked. The rest of the time, she kept mother's hours. She got up with and went to bed with the kids. During the day she puttered around Danny while keeping the baby occupied. After school she covered homework, special assignments, and dinner. Danny and Max often joined them for dinner. After dinner Danny would leave for the day, and Max would either work or spend quality time with the kids.

In this fashion Leslie became a fixture in the Baer household. After a successful month-long trial, she signed an annual work contract with Max. She agreed to revisit the decision to be a live-in nanny each summer after school got out. But, Leslie admitted to herself, she couldn't see ever wanting to leave.

Max has gracefully and without restrictions allowed me to mother his babies. I can certainly spend even the next ten years taking care of them. The only limit to this decision in Leslie's mind stemmed from the single problem she'd encountered. She would not stay once Max re-married. She'd gone so far as to put that in their contract. Max had seemed to accept her argument that he wouldn't need a nanny anymore if he obtained a wife. But the real reason remained unsaid. Leslie couldn't stay living in Max's house once he'd brought another woman into it. She'd begun to pray that she wasn't in love with him, but could not deny that she found him most attractive.

Leslie put the vacuum away and then with Janie in her chest carrier went down to the laundry room to tackle the first loads of clean laundry she'd washed the night before. She often stood like this, in Max's bedroom folding his socks and underwear and wishing she shared this room, this bureau, and this life fully with him.

As she moved on to Angie's room, she resolved again to focus on her life as it was. *You can do this. Spend each day taking care of these five precious kids until they grow up. They are the only kids you will ever have and so focus on them. Their father is out of your league, girl.*

★★★

Max came into the kitchen after dropping off his kids for their various Saturday night activities. The Sunday edition was done early, so instead of spending time at the paper as a family, he'd let his girls go stay the night with their maternal grandma, while he dropped the twins off at a friend's house for an all-night video game party.

He was looking forward to a quiet night with Janie and Leslie. He smiled as he thought about it. Often he'd urge Leslie to take the rare night off by farming out the older kids and taking care of the baby so she could leave. Usually, she'd go out doing heaven knows what, but would come back with a fun story or a bit of sparkle in her eye. And, sometimes, she'd choose to stay home and would hover around the house or even hang out in the same room with him enjoying a quiet night at home.

He wondered what she would choose to do tonight. With the kids staying out, she could probably go for the night and not come back until late tomorrow. He dropped off his briefcase on the dining room sideboard and then started looking for Leslie. On Saturdays he knew she liked to get the last of the laundry done from where Danny left off. So, he started downstairs in the laundry room. No luck. He then went through the rest of the downstairs looking for her. Eventually he made his way upstairs and followed the quiet sound of Leslie humming to Janie to the boys' room. He found her sitting on the lower bunk bed matching tube socks while she talked to a smiling and kicking baby Janie laying on the bed next to her.

She wasn't wearing makeup as usual and it seemed like she didn't know that Max had a weakness for makeup-less women. Both his mother and wife had had sensitive skin and couldn't wear makeup, so he'd learned how to appreciate a woman's natural beauty. He got away with watching her for nearly five minutes before she turned and saw him.

"Oh hi, Max. You're home early."

He moved from leaning against the door to come over and look down at her and Janie, "Yeah. The edition went early today, so I dropped the girls off at Grandma March's and the boys off at Nate's. Everyone is sleeping over, so I'll fetch the girls around noon and pick up the boys on the way home." He looked away from Janie to meet Leslie's gaze, "So what wild and crazy thing did you find to do to keep busy while I was out?"

Leslie smiled, "Janie and I vacuumed the TV room and have folded and put away all the laundry. We're a couple of wild and crazy girls."

Max laughed, "Well the kids are gone tonight, so you can take off if you like. I can take care of Janie and things until five tomorrow." He waited for her answer as he plotted how to introduce his *real* plans for the evening.

"Well, Katy has a cold, so I don't have anyone to visit tonight. If it's okay with you, I'd like to just hang out here."

Max nodded, ready to put his plan into action, "I was hoping you'd say that. See, I've been hankering for a steak dinner, and while I can certainly broil one, I'd be pleased to broil two and treat you to a steak dinner here at home. That is, unless you'd rather go out with one of your boyfriends."

Leslie laughed at their long-standing joke, "Oh sure, any one of my many boyfriends is home at seven PM on a Saturday night waiting for my call. After eating what the kids eat all week, I'd love to eat a steak with you."

"Good, it's settled. I'll take Janie down and get dinner started while you do what you need to up here." With that, Max scooped up his cooing baby girl and headed downstairs. The whole time, he was thinking, *I wonder if Leslie will count this as a date. I hope so.* Max whistled as he went. Leslie didn't know it, but he'd purposely cleared his schedule for tonight and Sunday in the hope he could convince her to let go of her nanny duties and see him as a man, not her boss.

★★★

Leslie tried to stop her hands from shaking nervously as usual as she matched the last of the twins' socks. *It's just dinner, a family dinner at that. It's just Max and Janie and you. You have nothing to be nervous about.* But, her nerves overwhelmed her. Lately, her resolve to keep Max at arms length and treat him as just her boss was getting harder and harder. *It doesn't help that he treats me like a member of the family. The man has no boundaries.* Leslie admitted the truth to herself. Max treated her just like he treated his other staff, as members of his extended newspaper family. *He treats me as if I'm a bit more than an employee, but not quite as if I could be his wife.* She thought sadly.

Leslie ran a brush through her hair and realized she hadn't brushed her teeth that morning. Hurriedly she brushed them as she wondered whether she should change clothes. She had to face the reality of her situation. She wasn't sure she could stay just working for Max. She wanted to keep doing all she was doing, but add loving Max to her list of daily chores. *Face it girl, you're probably already in love with him. You were attracted to his dark good looks the day you met him, and now, you're buried neck deep in his life and are happy about it. You'd even do this job for free. You have to face facts.* But, Leslie wasn't ready to face those facts. If she did, she'd have to leave, and she couldn't abandon the babies.

A run through her closet brought up a lacy pink sweater she loved. Leslie stripped out of the slightly ragged sweatshirt she'd been wearing for a silk top and the sweater. She told herself the earrings would improve her mood, while the lip-gloss happened to match the sweater. She prayed for courage as she went down the stairs.

★★★

Max had Janie in her highchair by the sink as he worked on the dry rub for the steaks. He'd bought two New York strips on the way home. The baby vegetable salad was already in the fridge waiting for the dressing he had mixed, and the seed potatoes were already baking in their drizzle of spices and olive oil. He'd snuck in some pralines and cream ice cream, Leslie's favorite, for dessert. It was tucked into the back of the freezer waiting for the right moment.

He plopped the steaks down to broil and was washing his hands when Leslie entered the kitchen. As always she looked beautiful to him. He noted the nice sweater and silk blouse, as well as the lip-gloss and freshly made hair. *If not a date, Leslie did dress up. Very promising.*

Leslie smiled and blushed faintly when she arrived. "Can I get some Cheerios® for Janie?"

"Sure, I was going to, but wanted to wait until I had washed my hands, but you can."

Once Leslie loaded Janie's tray, she stood a bit apart from Max looking uncomfortable. Max moved past her and grabbed Janie's chair. "Let's move you two over to the table." He wheeled Janie with one hand as he gently pushed Leslie with the other. At the table, he settled Janie to the left of his chair, and then sat Leslie in the chair to the right of his. "You'll notice I wanted us to have a quiet, intimate meal, so I took out the table leaves."

"Just the three of us?"

"Yup. Just me and my girls." Max turned away at that moment purposely. He wanted to give Leslie time to process his words. He didn't want to scare her, but he needed to see if the longing he'd seen in her eyes lately was what he thought it was.

He came back to the table with some of the fancy napkins they used at special meals like Thanksgiving. He laid an ivory napkin by the side of his plate and then Leslie's before he met her eyes. Her eyes were opened big, but she still hadn't said anything. He decided to get her talking to see if he could get them past this halfway life they'd begun. "What? Did I say something wrong? Why are you looking at me like that?"

"You said 'my girls.' It's just Janie and me tonight. What did you mean?"

Max grinned. *It's all going to plan. Here's my chance, finally.* "I meant what I said. You are both my girls." He came closer to Leslie and leaned down to say, "Janie's my girl, obviously, and well, lately I've been thinking of you, Miss Leslie, as my girl too." He looked deeply in her eyes for a moment and said, "That is, if you want to be." He thought, *Now or never.* and leaned in to kiss Leslie on the lips.

She kissed him back. Boy did she kiss him back. When he came to his senses, Max looked to his left and saw Janie staring at them. He felt Leslie's hands on his neck and turned his face back to her. "So, does that mean you'll be my girl, Les?"

Leslie looked dazed, but then she smiled and it lit her whole face. With a sparkle in her eyes, she answered, "Yes, Max. I'd give everything to be one of your girls."

She went to kiss him again, but he halted her slightly, and then stood them both up. He looked over to Janie, and said, "You may get tired of seeing this, baby girl." as he pulled Leslie against the hard length of his body and enveloped her in his arms. Looking at Leslie, but speaking still to Janie he said, "I love this girl and I'll be kissing her a lot for a long time." And then he kissed Leslie again.

The shrill chirping of the smoke alarms was followed closely by Danny's opening of the kitchen door. Danny yelled, "Where's the fire?" His shout alerted Max and Leslie to the alarms and the fact that they had maybe kissed a little too long.

Max opened a window and then the stove to let the smoke out, while Leslie moved Janie into fresh air. They both couldn't stop laughing enough to answer Danny's questions about why the fire alarms were going off in his apartment's keypad connected to the house's security system.

Max regained some control first, telling Danny, "Call us in some Chinese delivery. I'll fill you in over some pot stickers." He then winked at Leslie who blushed.

Danny looked at her and then back at Max and shook his head, "It's about time you two hooked up. I am just glad you cleared the alert before the fire trucks got here."

Then they all realized Max had forgot to cancel the fire alarm when they heard sirens coming from down the street. The three burst into laughter again. Things were going to be just fine in the Baer household.

About the Author

Virginia Babcock has always loved romantic fiction, and now writes her own stories of love and life in the real world. Virginia lives in northern Utah where she works full-time when she's not writing books. Her husband and cat keep her constantly entertained the rest of the time.